Dancing on Sloane Street

To

All my love
English Golsworthy
A.K.A. Eve

To the child in all of us........

Every child is an artist. The problem is how to remain an artist once you grow up.

—Pablo Picasso.

Chapter 1

Written whilst listening to 'The Waters of March' by Antonio Carlos Jobim

April 27th 1996, 2.45pm, Ladbroke Grove, West London (the flat)

'Hello.' I answered in a less than enthusiastic tone.

'It's Pattie, how are we today?'

Pattie was my booker. God, her condescending tone made me want to shoot myself or better still, someone else. I took a moment for composure and then managed to answer in the appropriate manner: 'I'm well, Pattie, thank you for asking, and yourself?' My voice was starting to rise up at the end of the sentence as I knew full well she was anything but fine and really wanted to rip my silly little head off.

I held the receiver as far away from my ear as humanly possible in anticipation of the onslaught I knew was coming.

'What the bloody hell were you thinking English?' She always started off like this, and then would get progressively louder. 'I mean, WHY?! For heaven's sake!'

'I thought that's what you wanted,' I answered very quietly.

'Hang on a minute.' She cleared her throat and I heard her light up one of the Marlboro Reds that would be sitting on her desk, handy for one of our little chats. 'You thought' - she paused for dramatic effect - 'that Wilkinson Sword, suppliers of razors to Middle England, wanted you, the model, in a bathtub, naked, with some Brazilian girl shaving your nonny?'

Mmhmm, I thought for a second... now that she put it like that, it didn't sound so promising, no...

'It wasn't my idea, that's what he asked me to do,' I protested. 'The photographer.'

'Look, Yossi Popoladoplas is Yossi Popoladoplas, I agree' - she took another inhalation – 'but when he locked the ad people out of the bathroom - you know, the people you were supposedly working for - didn't you stop to think that perhaps, possibly, this was not exactly the type of picture that they wanted to advertise their new Lady Shave razor?'

I said nothing. It had been my first big booking of the season, an advertising job for Wilkinson Sword, and it was being shot by Yossi, the iconic fashion photographer. I had no idea why Wilkinson wanted to use Popoladoplas, whose photographs are... well, difficult. They have a veneer of violence and voyeurism, and almost always feature nudes. How this would have worked with Wilkinson's brand I had no idea, but the ad agency obviously thought it was a genius idea.

They flew me out to Monte Carlo after a quick pit stop in Milan. When we touched down in the south of France I was summoned to meet "The Master". After a few Polaroid's and a quick look at my body (this is the norm with Yossi) he seemed quite happy to shoot me for the ad. What he neglected to tell the ad men was he was only willing to photograph me in his bathtub completely naked with an equally naked Brazilian girl shaving my muff.

We went ahead with the shoot as planned, but Yossi decided to lock the now livid ad executives out of the bathroom of his home while he shot me and the Brazilian chick naked in a blue water-filled bathtub in some very provocative positions, with his very strange wife sitting in the corner of the room wearing a blue anorak.

Needless to say, the pictures got banned from publication and Wilkinson Sword never requested to work with either me or Popoladoplas again.

Wilkinson Sword was supposed to be my big break. In the hierarchy of the model world, an ad campaign takes you to a new level.

There are two sorts of models you see... the shit ones (catalogue) and the good ones (editorial). Catalogue models are merely pretty and inoffensive and end up on things like Plumbing World calendars looking pretty and inoffensive. Editorial models spend a lot of time gaining editorial credits usually in secondary markets first, like Milan, then in London and New York. Editorial pay is shit though. The goal is to use the editorial credits to get a nice, fat, ad campaign like Wilkinson Sword, for instance. I was being fast-tracked with the Wilkinson ads because my book wasn't that strong yet and Pattie was reminding me I had really messed it up.

What was left unsaid was that I was 17 and washed up as a model.

Pattie tried a different tack: 'I mean, please, what you were thinking in that bath tub? I'd really like to know?'

I started to clear my throat, trying to decide whether to tell her the truth or make up a lie that would make her less angry. I finally decided on the truth.

'I was thinking about his house. I'd never been to the South of France before and his bathroom was just amaz...' She butted in, 'Truly amazing', and took another inhalation of her Marlboro Red. For reasons I've never understood, all bookers smoke Marlboro Red, perhaps to show how tough they are. By contrast, all models smoke Marlboro Lights. Perhaps that's to demonstrate their more delicate side. There seemed to be no variation on this theme.

'You've really outdone yourself this time haven't you? Forever pushing the boundaries of stupidity, aren't we?'

Well, now that she mentioned it, yes I supposed that could be a fair description of my behaviour of late.

'Look, just a word of advice.'

'Yes,' I answered, as sweetly as was possible for me, glad to put an end to this little chit chat.

'Every time you speak it gets worse. From now on, do not get into any more situations, and try to be a bit smarter, that's all. OK, can we manage that?'

There she goes again, condescending. 'OK Pattie,' I answered, in an equally annoying tone. 'I'll try, OK?'

She put the phone down first. I slowly followed, glad that was over with. *Anyway, he did have an amazing house. I don't care what she says. It was worth it, just to be in his house. In fact one day I'm going to live over there, in the south of France. I'm going to move to the south of France.*

I slowly got up from the chair and headed to the kitchen to make some toast. We were not meant to eat bread - it bloats you - but there was nothing else here and I was sick to death of this monastic lifestyle, so I just ate it, regardless. I stopped to have a look out the kitchen window to remind myself of why I was here.

I never wanted to be a model – it was a dumb ass way to earn a living if you ask me, not that I was particularly intelligent or anything but honestly, unless you were one of the supermodels, it wasn't fun and it wasn't cool. You only heard about the winners in the industry.

All the others - about 99 % of models - were earning a pittance... but if they still had the brains they were born with (most of them don't) they almost certainly had their own little hustle on the side – you had to or else you were nothing but a high class slave, forever indebted to your agency.

Work on a daily basis was a series of rejections, or humiliations: 'Hello sweetie, we'd just like you to dance round in this tiny G-string bikini while we spray you with water and all you have to do is tell the camera how much you like this lame ass product we're trying to sell.... in Turkish, if you can. OK, sweetie?' and that was one of the better jobs.

My Milan apartment consisted of cockroaches, the odd transvestite hooker and eastern European girls living off baby food. You were always waiting for that one big job to come and it never flipping did. Much like the art world, the rewards were so disproportionate to the talent involved, you ended up feeling like a wotless idiot anyway, regardless of whether you won or lost.

I'd always wanted to live in the City, that was the plan anyway, even from a young age. Yes, the countryside was alright, full of trees and things, but I wanted to see life from another perspective: experience the sights and sounds of unfamiliarity, meet new people to hang out with, upset and annoy.

That hadn't been too difficult until last week, when after a minor misdemeanour at a fashion party (Mick, remember me?), I got put under a sort of unofficial house arrest by the agency. Come the evening, the furthest I could venture out of the apartment was to the bottom of the street. Or I could have gone upstairs, which would have meant visiting the retired rock star that lived above us, someone called Mojo, I think, apparently responsible for that hideous song Dienna. At the time I had no idea there was some lame band around called Mojovox, stupid name if you ask me. Anyway, Mojo would sometimes invite us up when he was having one of his shindigs, hardly ever, but sometimes.

Other times we needed to borrow a pair of sharp scissors from him, to cut away the small grey mushrooms that grew from the living room carpet. Such was the damp in the apartment that if all of us went away for any length of time (there were three of us) these strange little things would start to sprout. Then we'd have to cut them away, dry the offending patch with a hairdryer and hope for the best. Had we not removed them regularly, we might have had a lucrative side line in mushroom farming.

The main bedroom was shared with another 17 year-old model named Crystal. Two mattresses on the floor, a wicker wardrobe on my side of the room, and a tiny bedside table which lived on Crystal's side of the room. On this perched a Mickey Mouse alarm clock with the loudest alarm I had ever heard.

Crystal's mattress was pulled up next to the window, which was unfortunate as the window had no curtain or blind. It looked out onto Cambridge Gardens, the tree-lined street below. In the other bedroom was Kelly. Kelly was also my age and was from the countryside too, we had the same mannerisms. She liked the same foods as I did - rice on toast, for example - we would laugh at the same jokes, our un-placeable accents were quite similar.

But she had something I didn't: an ever-increasing coke habit.

Kelly would fund this habit by raiding the large grey payphone that had been installed in the hallway by the agency. This contraption would not have looked out of place in the local YMCA, and it gobbled up money faster than Kelly's nose could hoover up coke - just as well, really, as she'd take a hammer to it every other weekend, breaking the massive padlock and emptying the money out.

The best time for her to attack the phone would be after Crystal's weekend call to her mother in Utah, when it was loaded with coins. However, that wasn't always possible because Billy, Kelly's dealer, would always call round whenever he was short of cash.

On one occasion, a loud noise jolted me out of my sleep. It was the early hours of Thursday morning and I'd not long been in bed as the rocker upstairs was having one of his parties, which meant there would be loud beats of sound penetrating through his floor boards and our ceiling. Only Crystal with her 'magic pills' - which she got raiding her mother's prescription meds cabinet on her annual trips back to Utah - would be able to sleep through it, but on this occasion, the rocker was not the only one keeping me awake.

It must have been around 3.30am when I finally got up to investigate the incessant noise coming from the pavement outside. I made my way over to Crystal's side of the room and the window looking out onto the street so I could find out what all the noise was about.

'Oy, you lot, I know you're in there!' came the big booming man's voice echoing off into the night. 'One of you owes me money, yeah? I want it tonight, yeah?'

Oh fuck! I started to think, she may have got away with it in the past but tonight it looked like Billy meant business. Someone had to do something quick as the elderly couple who lived opposite were bound to call the police.

I jumped over Crystal's mattress and pulled up the wooden window with the bottom handle. Both hands, it was heavy. 'Billy,' I half whispered and half shouted. My eyes were scanning around, surveying the shadows. A lanky figure in a green anorak started to step out from behind a broad willowy oak tree on the other side of the road.

'Just give me the money she owes me and I'm off,' he growled up at me, voice still booming out into the darkness.

He started to pace up and down, perhaps agitated, or perhaps just high on his own supply. Not sure which. It was at that moment I heard banging and stumbling around coming from the hallway. *This can't be happening...*

I went into the hallway and there was Kelly, down on her hands and knees, hammer in hand, emptying out what looked like the entire payphone. There was enough small change surrounding her on the floor to feed a small Third World village for a week.

'Quick, help me bag it up,' she whispered to me, her voice shaky. 'Come on Kathy, help, please.' 'Kathy?' I looked around in bewilderment, 'Who the hell is Kathy?' I asked. Then it suddenly dawned on me that when you've taken that much blow at this stupid o'clock in the morning, you're really past caring what the hell anyone's name is. But really, even by my uniquely liberal standards of behaviour this was pushing it...

We started to scoop up the piles of coins and load the change into a Tesco carrier. 'This is the last time,' I said, shaking my head in disbelief. 'This bullshit has to stop.'

'It will, I promise, Kathy,' Kelly answered while trying to tie a knot in the bag. 'It'll never happen again.'

So we carried the full bag of coins over to the still open window, climbed over comatosed Crystal, being careful not to stand on her, and hurled the now bursting Tesco bag with all our might out of the window and into the starry night sky...

Chapter 2

Written whilst listening to 'Gangsta's Paradise' by Coolio

June 23rd, 3.45 p.m., West London

I woke up to a pounding head and a bad need to get out of the dingy agency apartment.
I decided to take a stroll to clear my brain as I seemed to be recovering from the last vestiges of flu I'd had the week before. I also wanted to get away from the most mindlessly listless conversations that my roommate Crystal would start upon returning from visiting her parents in Utah. These would get increasingly moronic as the day progressed.

From what I could gather her family were strict Mormons, would you believe, and quite concerned about what models got up to in their downtime from work whilst living in a city like London. They should have asked me. I would have reassured them that they had nothing to worry about as their little angel was more than happy to stay home, paint her toenails and discuss the possibility of her one day being regarded as the most beautiful woman in the world, whilst staring blankly into space having taken her daily dose of prescription meds stolen from her mother's medicine cabinet on her departure to London. Nothing to worry about at all.

My walk from the flat took me through Holland Park, down Kensington High Street, up a little alleyway past the cigarette shop, Marks and Spencer and the Big Issue seller, coming out just a little way up from Harrods on the other side of the road. Burberry was on the corner.

I knew Burberry designs because I had done a show for them. It was a shitty show and I looked fat in all the clothes. I knew I looked fat in the clothes as they kept telling me so. Fashion people, lovely folk they are, honestly...

But anyway I crossed over the road and made my way towards Sloane Street, the London equivalent of Beverly Hills, some might say (usually the blind) but anyway, they did have the kind of shops you could only gaze at and dream as an outfit from one of them would bankrupt you. Even the notion of trying something on would remind you of society's divisions and what side you were on, or not on. The right price can buy you all this, should you desire it.

And I did. Desire it, I mean. That and much, much more.

Lots of girls around my age didn't know what they wanted. They were confused, hopping from one dead-end relationship to the next, staying in uninspiring unfulfilling jobs with no sense of what they truly were or what they were doing there behind the crisp white, ill-fitting, unimaginative uniform, the kind that would drain the spirit from your soul and sap any form of spontaneity from your now overweight and lethargic body. Living like this would institutionalise even the most wondrous of minds into a formless, conformist lump of shit that would please only middle-aged relatives, civil servants and the self-interested government that had made you take that desperate, God-forsaken job in the first place.

This is not how I intended to live. Surely there had to be more to life than that? I couldn't stop thinking about it, all too often now, on a daily basis in fact, and ok I'd not got a bad deal so far however, there was a whole world out there for the taking and I wanted it - all of it, and that's when I met her. Mimi.

I was just about to turn on my heels and head home. My feet ached and so did my brain. Sloane Street's quite exhausting with no money.

The sky was turning from a blue grey to a dull afternoon gloom. I had just enough loose change in my pocket for a burger. You know, one of those shitty, cheap extra processed kinds you could pick up for 99p from most of the cheap chicken shops on the way home and Crystal wanted me to pick up her usual large strawberry milkshake, with extra milk.

Standing in the doorway of the Alberta Ferretti dress shop, I paused to light my last Marlboro Light when I realised I'd lost my Zippo lighter. Damn, it must have been at the opening of that health food store I'd popped into that morning on Westbourne Grove. Bugger. I started to rummage around in my oversized model bag. *Oh come on, there must be some matches in here somewhere! I carry every other motherfucking thing in this bag; why not a match?* Just as I thought I'd located one there came a voice from the pavement beside me: 'You really shouldn't be smoking, you know, young lady. It does terrible things to your skin.'

'Who the fuck are you?' I exclaimed before having a look round to see exactly which dumbass was telling me how to live my life and immediately regretted my choice of words, as the women standing in front of me was certainly no dumb-ass. In fact she was probably one of the most strikingly sophisticated women I had ever seen in my life and she definitely did not look like the type who would be prepared to take lip from me that day.

'Oh, I didn't see you there,' I apologised. 'You don't have a light do you?' I pretended not to have heard what she'd said to me about smoking two seconds before. She reached into her pocket and pulled out a long thin elegant box of matches: you know, the type with the white tip that you'd probably get given free in one of these high end clothing stores that the average person could barely afford to dip her toe into, let alone buy something.

I thanked her, accepting the match and lit up hoping she was going to leave soon so I could smoke myself into an early grave in peace. No such luck. She was still standing there. I took a long, slow inhalation whilst turning to my reflection in the window of the shop. I could see that she was looking at me as well, her eyes pouring over every inch of my face, studying my features, like an artist studying a sculpture to make sure every single line, curve and proportion was just perfect. As I turned back towards the street, she reached a hand out to meet mine.

'Mimi,' she announced, giving my hand a squeeze. 'You must be a model; you look malnourished and you're wearing second-hand clothes. Dead giveaway. Christ, were those trousers supposed to be white?' she added in bewilderment.

I tried to force a laugh, however I really wanted to out my ciggy on her face 'Yes, a model,' I replied. 'A more or less unemployed one at the moment, not that it bothers me,' I went on nonchalantly. 'I really want to be a writer, but you know, the usual shortcomings, lack of brain power, huge lapses in concentration, lack of education, I could go on.'

'Oh,' she laughed. 'My favourite kind.'

I'm not quite sure what she meant by that but had a horrible feeling I was just about to find out. 'Look, I don't bat for the other team, if that's what you're after. Sorry.' I tried not to give her too much eye contact.

'Nor do I, darling; that's not my interest at all. Look,' she exclaimed, pointing at her very expensive watch. 'It's past lunch, I'm starving. I live in Chelsea, and that's not far in a cab from here. Come on. You look as though you could do with a little advice from someone like moi, and I've just bought too much fish for supper. You might as well come and join me.' We both stopped for a second in complete silence. 'Oh, come on. You've got nothing to lose. I don't bite, and by the look of things, you do.'

She was probably right, I thought to myself; if it came to it, I'm sure she would come off worse. Crystal's milkshake could wait, and fish would no doubt top my burger. It was no contest really. 'OK,' I announced, 'but I smoke a lot, I like to swear and I am also of the opinion that a meal without wine is like a day without sunshine. OK?'

'Oh shut it,' she replied, 'firstly, we live in England where sunshine is hardly plentiful and secondly, you are not Joan bloody Collins, OK? But I may have some wine somewhere...' And with that she let out a chuckle, whipped her cashmere shawl around her shoulders and smoothed down her expensively highlighted hair. Off we went while she applied a fresh coat of Chanel lippy. She steered in the direction of Harrods to find a cab.

Now it was my turn to study her as she stood just a few feet away from me with her arm out in the middle of the street trying to hail a taxi. There was something vaguely

European and slightly aristocratic about her. I started to wonder what she could possibly want with me. We finally found a cab, which was good timing as it was starting to spot with rain and she had the appearance of someone who certainly couldn't tolerate rain.

In a mist of her Chanel Number Five we quickly scuttled into the cab. 'Chelsea darling' she said to the driver and off we went. We were taking the back streets to avoid the traffic. We went past Chelsea and Westminster Hospital and pulled up to a little house in a cobbled mews not far from the hospital itself: number 27 with a yellow door.

I could already hear dogs yapping as we walked to the door - at least two of them, I guessed. Small dogs too, like the Queen's Corgis. She turned to me: 'I hope you like dogs... Hum... what was your name again?' she asked.

'Jackie,' I said, just making up the first name that came into my head.

'Oh, yes', she said, 'sorry. I knew it began with a -j.' She didn't, but I let her get away with it anyway.

When we went into her house, the dogs bounded on us – small, yappy, white things - Shih Tzu I thought. I also began to realise that though the house looked small from the outside that was totally deceiving.

Once you got inside, it opened up to mansion-like proportions. It was gracefully decorated, with beautifully intricate chandeliers and a few silver-framed photographs dotted around the walls. The living room was to the left; straight ahead was a statue of Socrates leading down the stairs to the marble-clad, off-white kitchen; the kitchen opened up to patio doors draped in lemon and white linen, leading out to a small grass garden studded with white and pink frangipanis, surrounded by a 1960s style wall - probably to keep prying eyes out.

I liked it and she could tell. She turned to me with a cheeky smile. 'You can even sunbathe naked in the summer, darling. No one can see. It's totally private.'

I might just take her up on the offer, I thought to myself; it's not far from my place on the tube and there's certainly nowhere to sunbathe naked there. She handed me a large glass of rosé wine. As a joke, she had put heart-shaped pink ice cubes and some sort of edible flower on the top. This woman made me laugh, I thought to myself as I took a sip. Mmhmm... Not bad wine either.

We knocked back the rosé in about 45 minutes and then Mimi opened another bottle. I helped myself to a packet of Marlboro Lights she had in a bowl in the living room, along with other brands of cigarettes and some sweets – for guests I suppose (what a good hostess).

I noticed that her left hand, which was clutching the wine, was wedding band free, but she didn't strike me as the kind of woman who worked. Born into it, maybe, but I wasn't quite sure; she had an air of mystique about her and the self-assurance of someone quite capable of running the show on her own. I couldn't work out her age - maybe late 30s?

She emptied her shopping out onto the table in the vague hope of working out what to cook. It was early evening now and I for one had started feeling distinctly light-headed after two bottles of wine and no lunch. By the looks of things she felt the same way, giggling slightly at her lack of coordination, and had seemed to throw her meal plans out the window. Or was that me being there? Then the phone went.

'Sorry, darling, I'm going to have to answer this.' She trotted up to the top of the stairs near the entrance hall. I moved over to stand just beside the lamp at the bottom of the stairs, well within earshot. She's wasn't very happy about something by the sound of it.

I decided to have a quick snoop in the cupboard next to me before she returned to the room. A warm gust of Hermes scent hit me as I opened it, but to my surprise there was nothing much in there other than a vintage Chanel handbag, two discarded plane tickets, a leopard print G-string (*that can't be hers*) and a bottle of very expensive champagne, Cristal by the looks of it. I then wandered over to the book shelf, on the other side of the room near the dining table.

What have we here... I thought. Some kind of feminist by the looks of things, for there seemed to be an overwhelming number of books written by the type of women most men are terrified of: Simone De Beauvoir, Germaine Greer and... there were other writers too: Dante Alighieri, W.B. Yeats, Henry Fielding and William Shakespeare were names I recognised. I took another listen to the conversation upstairs.

Mimi was trying to arrange a dinner date between someone by the name of Money and a girl called India at Blake's Hotel in Chelsea but India was indisposed because of excessive alcohol consumption. Then the line went dead. 'Hello, hello... Bugger, I've lost her.' I heard Mimi announce.

In my naivety I assumed she was running some sort of dating agency and left it at that. I could hear her coming back down the stairs so I quickly glided across her newly polished glossy parquet floor, being careful not to make a sound and gently plonked down my rather tatty bag next to her dainty rosewood coffee table, while at the same time plonking my arse down on the only available chair with a view of the garden, hoping to give the impression I was having a quiet contemplative moment to myself. She wasn't buying it for a second.

'So go on. How much did you hear then?' she abruptly

questioned me.

'Hear what? I don't know what you mean. But your garden is quite lovely...'

'Oh cut the crap,' she sighed, pouring us both more wine. 'What kind of men do you like?'

'What? What are you talking about?' I knew full well what she was talking about but needed to stall for time. I thought for a second. 'I mean, in what kind of context?'

'In every context. OK, give me an example of your boyfriends over the last few years.'

'Well,' I answered gamely, 'mostly musicians...'

'Annnnnd,' she butted in, 'mostly homeless, right?'

'Well, not entirely,' I said, trying to defend it. 'But some of them were on community service.'

She almost choked on her heart shaped ice cube. 'Oh come on, darling, that's ridiculous. It's not good for you, me or the economy. This has to change and I have a plan. What time is it? Ok, 10 to 7. You pop upstairs, first room on the left, walk-in wardrobe to the right, choose anything you'd like to wear, we're around the same size, then pop back downstairs and show me what it looks like.'

'Is there any point to this? I mean, I think we can safely establish you have lots of money and I don't, and my wearing some of your very expensive clothes is not really going to change that very much.'

'That's where you're wrong,' she went on. 'Play your cards right and things could be very different for you. I hope you don't have to be anywhere this evening?'

'If I did, it looks like I'm not going to make it, doesn't it?' She smiled, pulled out a moleskin notepad and started to call a number from it.

I dutifully made my way upstairs, kicking my shoes off and leaving them at the bottom. Once inside her boudoir-style bedroom I really did have my pick of the best: Chanel, Herrera, Joseph, Burberry... which was funny... *By the looks of things, I may not even need another booking from them with this chick on-side.* I eventually decided on an Alberta Ferretti number, as that was a style I had always been able to pull off. It was long and flowing and I knew it would suit me. I had done some fittings for them during the London shows and loved the clothes.

I looked in the mirror. Wowser*! I seemed very young, her clothes were so sophisticated I looked like a child in them.* I opened up the top drawer on the armoire and found some black Chanel eye make-up next to some diamond earrings. Deciding to leave the earrings alone, I picked up the black eye pencil and outlined my eyes carefully and then went back down. At the foot of the stairs was a brand new pair of Jimmy Choos. I put them on. They were slightly too small, but I was used to wearing ill-fitting shoes as I'm always borrowing other peoples (blame the economy).

I went into the kitchen; Mimi was just wrapping things up on the phone: 'It's just dinner. Remember she's a beginner, darling.' Then she hung up and beckoned me over, arms outstretched. 'I knew it!' she gushed, pointing me in the direction of a full length mirror. 'Now this is how a woman is supposed to look.'

The dress was split to the thigh, exposing the whole of my leg at times; the front of the dress was high to my neck with tiny little straps that reached all the way down my back, leaving most of it exposed. In my opinion it all looked far too in your face to be classed as elegant, but that had always been my problem. I did seem to make everything look a bit rude, even if it wasn't necessarily the intention. Mimi was smiling now so broadly anyone would have thought she had just rescued an entire third world country from poverty.

She plucked out two crystal champagne flutes from her drinks cabinet and then went to the cupboard by the stairs, the one I had been snooping in earlier, pulling out the bottle of champers. 'I'd been saving this,' she said, opening it up with great haste and handing me a glass. It was warm, but that didn't matter. She glanced at her watch, 'Oh we don't have much time. Let's make a toast: champagne to my real friends, and real pain to my sham friends.' With that we clinked and sipped our respective glasses. My hands were slightly shaking and there was a pounding in my chest; good or bad, I was unsure at this point, but something in my heart was telling me I had just made a deal with the devil herself.

I didn't want to go by cab; Blake's Hotel was only down the road but Mimi insisted. I would already be late, even if I left that instant, so we didn't have time to waste. She grabbed her coat and I a small clutch bag, on loan of course, containing only my phone, her telephone number and the box of Marlboro Lights I had nicked from her. To ask her for a suitable coat to wear would have most certainly been pushing my luck. Anyway, I'd only have to remove it again inside.

'Now what have I told you?' she asked. I gave her a brief recap: 'no smoking, no swearing, no smutty jokes and oh yeah, don't forget the envelope'. 'That bit's crucial', she went on; 'do not forget the fucking envelope darling, OK?' 'OK.' I replied, more concerned about the not smoking and not swearing parts at this point.

The cab pulled over and I got in.

'Oh and one more thing, darling heart. It's about India. This was her... hum... project originally, but I didn't count on her getting her arse here on time. However you are far better suited for this one - him I mean - you are far better suited for him. In fact I think he'll fall in love with you but you need to get him on-side and the other chick out of the picture if you want to win this one, and let me tell you something. This one's worth winning. Long term. A possible keeper. Whatever needs to be done, do it.'

She then swiftly kisses my left cheek, carefully closes the taxi door and I was on my own. Off to the world of professional bullshit by the sounds of things, and something told me I might be good at it. Very good indeed.

I had never been to Blake's before. It was a refined, special hotel used by the cognoscenti and the occasional film star. The exterior was painted black and there were no loud, vulgar signs inviting the uninvited to enter.

I got into the hotel, and India and Money were seated downstairs in the small restaurant, as Mimi had told me. I could see them from the lobby.

Her, well, let's start with her: mid-twenties I'd say, tall, sleek and expensive looking with an overall air of rebellion to match, like a reborn Bettie Page, far too perfect to be interesting too. Girls like her didn't need to try, I should know, trust me, I lived with them.

And him, well, this is when I stopped in my tracks: he was stylish to say the least, dressed in mostly back with his shirt buttoned up to the neck, without a tie. He didn't need it with that dapper sense of ease with himself; he could have worn anything and gotten away with it. Fluid and poetic were his movements with a kind of face that would be easy to fall in love with, that's for sure, with an enigmatic smile, intriguingly smokey eyes and the physique of a professional athlete. But even from the stairs, it was his hands I noticed the most: they were tanned, with long fingers, elegant and refined, and there was a ring on his little finger of the left hand that would twinkled under the soft lighting. I couldn't take my eyes off him; there was just something about him...

The steps were steep leading down there, and what with the wine and the too small shoes it took the help of one rather sexy Greek waiter, as well as a handrail, to get me down without the humiliation of an arse over tit entrance.

Why I was in the highest, most dumbass shoes, as I certainly didn't need the height advantage, which now pushed me well over 6 foot, I couldn't fathom. Maybe Money really liked tall girls, but who gives a shit, I'm here to cause trouble, that's what I'm good at.

He stood up as I approached the table and the beautiful yet sulky India looked like she wanted to poke my eye out with a stick. *Oh, what fun!* I thought to myself and with a quick flick of the hips, I swiftly swept her Champagne Bellini off the table and downed the glass of bubbly as if I owned it, and thanked him for being such a sweetheart, with a hugely inappropriate kiss on his lips.

To do this I had to push myself part way between her, him and the table, shooting my arse out in her face as I bent down. She not surprisingly recoiled in horror while he, bemused and bewildered, looked on, half smiling but with nervous expectation. So he should have been nervous, for I was just getting started and with a body content of probably around 90% alcohol, anything could happen. We had a whole evening to get through and didn't India know it, for this was just my warm up act and there was plenty more where this came from.

I went to see the baby-faced waiter who had helped me down the stairs. I found him at the bar preparing some drinks. I helped myself to one of those whilst also instructing him we needed another chair at table 13. 'No problem' he replied. 'Oh and what's your name?' he asked. 'It's whatever you want it to be,' I replied, helping myself to another drink from his tray.

Then I went back to the table and stood while the waiter gently slid the chair in behind me. At this point, India excused herself and got up to go to the ladies. Bingo! I jumped up, pulled out her chair, which was right next to his, and plonked my drunken arse down next to him. 'Hello,' I said, picking up her now replaced drink and knocking that back too.

'You're very good at stealing drinks aren't you?' he said with a smile, while beckoning the waiter to bring us a bottle of Champagne.

'Yes, I learnt it in juvenile correctional facilities a few years back. Do you have any unusual talents?'

'Well,' he looked at me thoughtfully for a moment, 'I'm not bad at stealing police cars.'

I couldn't help but snigger. It wasn't a bad line from someone like him, I thought to myself.

'Not been in one of them for a while...'

'That's good to know.' he went on, 'you know, if we're going to become friends...' He was looking at me very carefully now, with his arm round the back of my chair.

At that moment India came back from the bathroom looking distinctly uncomfortable at the sight of the two of us together. So she should have been, for in that moment - don't ask me how - I just knew that everything was about to change. He wanted to hang out with me that much I could tell.

Oh no, the envelope! I'd completely forgotten. But when was I supposed to ask for it? What to do? I discreetly slid my hand into his suit jacket pocket and... Crap, it wasn't there. India was ever more distraught as she thought she just witnessed me trying to rob him. How dumb is this chick?

She then decided to make light conversation: 'So where are you from, Mr Money,' she purred, playing with her hair.

Oh Lord, give me strength; there's no way I can sit through hours of this.

I started to whisper at him through the side of my mouth. 'Where's the bloody envelope?'

'This is a joke. You don't ask for it yet,' he whispered back. 'That happens later, and until then you try to be a polite member of society. Do you think you can manage that?'

I pulled a face as much to say you'd have more luck getting a horse to talk. He read my mind and tried another tacked. 'Look kid...' He cleared his throat and looked me straight in the face 'I think I like you, OK, which is strange as I never really like anyone, business or personal. In my country, where I come from, I'm a highly respected person, OK? I have to be careful what I do. Now I may find your bullshit mildly amusing but plenty of people may not, so what I'm saying is.... '

'I know what you're saying,' I interrupted, 'and it's cool. I'll give it a go. I mean how bad can it be, right?' He looked at me sceptically, and then reached into his bag from under the table. He handed India a big brown envelope.

'It was lovely to meet you,' he said. 'I'll see you out' they both got up from the table and headed up the stairs to the entrance of the hotel.

I then rushed into my borrowed bag to text Mimi, but there was already a message on my phone from her. 'Whatever happens now is down to you. Be smart, be safe, and don't forget the bloody envelope darling. X'

Chapter 3

Written whilst listening to 'Suicidal Blonde' by INXS

Still June 1996, 11.15 a.m., West London.

I awakened to the smell of coco butter and cash, and unfortunately it was coming from me. What the hell was I doing last night? There were two fifty pound notes casually stuck to my leg and the rest of it tucked away in 'the envelope' which was neatly tucked away under my left armpit.

There was an international mobile number written across the envelope in what looked to be my handwriting with the name 'Mr. Money' scribbled next to it. With a mouth as dry as the Saudi desert itself I began to recall the events and happenings of the night and day before. Then I decided to dial the number.

I was met with a long dialing tone. *Oh here we go... he must answer, he has to.* He does. 'Hey kid, I'm in a meeting in Geneva but going to fly back to see you, tonight if I can. Do you miss me already?' 'Mmhmm' I replied, or something like that, thinking about the smell of his wallet. However, there was something I liked about him and not just financially – in a sort of foreign way, an unfamiliar spice I'd not tried before but could probably get the taste for, in the right quantities. My roommate Crystal had started to stir and I reassured him we would speak later before hanging up the phone.

Christ, you couldn't make this shit up, I thought to myself while reading a text just sent to me from Mimi. The instructions read: 'Drop off cash, shoes, and dress by noon today - oh and bring something to sun yourself in. Mimi.' What did she have planned for me now? I'd only just got rid of the last one!

I jumped up and sauntered to the agency apartment bathroom, which was not particularly salubrious, of course. I started to inspect the damage. *Well, not bad, considering*. My mascara-streaked face had a warm glow to it, but all the important bits were still in place - mostly the underwear. But what was that? Something was hanging down from behind my pants.

Before I could investigate further, Crystal came gliding into the bathroom, adrift on a mix of prescription meds. 'Well, I'm sure I ain't responsible for putting that there,' she announced in an American drawl, while peeling the £50 note from my skin, positioned, as far as I could make out, just below my left butt cheek.

'You can keep that,' I told her, feeling slightly guilty that I made her wait nine hours last night for a milkshake that obviously never materialized. I was also feeling safe in the knowledge that there was plenty more where that came from.

With that thought, I made my way into the kitchen to prepare my breakfast of half a grapefruit accompanied by a small sprinkle of sweetener on the top.

Crystal came over to join me in the kitchen clutching a raspberry flavored Pop Tart straight from the toaster. We sat in silence, her thinking about nothing much probably, and me taking in the events of last night. Then it hit me: this was not the way to do it. Over-thinking things, I mean.

I needed to get a clear perspective on exactly what it was that I was doing, or about to do. The whys, what ifs, justifications and condemnations could wait. I had been given an opportunity, perhaps a gift here, he really liked me, this Money guy, I could tell. I didn't need anyone else; this was my chance to see the world... me and Money, just the two of us.

I needed to act fast, think on my feet for a while. This modeling game is for mugs: any fool could tell you that. I couldn't stop here; this was just the beginning. I couldn't walk away from this now. Something felt right, he was my calling perhaps. Yet it wasn't the new money in my pocket that made me feel special, it was the way I'd go about getting it, it was its instant potential that gave me that rush.

It's all about the money I said to myself with a smile... *Oh the money!*

I was going to live the life that most people dreamed about and I was going to do it bigger and better than anyone had ever done it before... just watch me...!

A little after noon I was sitting smoking a Marlboro on the

doorstep of what can now be referred to as Miss Mimi's house in Chelsea.

The sun had finally broken through the clouds and I was basking in the mid-day heat. The only thoughts in my head were of a large chilled glass of Chardonnay, then an image of a private plane flying across the Atlantic came into my mind... I was wearing a floor length Chanel dress... I was somewhere exotic...

But then, with a heavy clunk, Mimi opened the door jolting me out of my daydream. She was dressed in a full-length Heidi Klein kaftan, covering what looked like a quite beautifully embroidered Missoni bikini.

'Come in, darling.'

She took me by the hand and led me down to her kitchen once again. We made ourselves comfortable around the table and without even so much of a hint of a glass of wine; she started to talk about Money.

'Now, Money will most definitely be preoccupied with business for the next few days so I thought it best if I lined up something else for you.' I was afraid this was coming. Money would have been more than enough for me to deal with, but she had other ideas. I let out a sigh and slumped down on the table, head in hands, being purposely over-dramatic.

'Go on, hit me with it,' I grumbled, not quite anticipating what was coming next.

'Well, his name is Al Hajji Cartoon. He owns a medium-sized country as well as many other things you might be interested in. At any rate, he'll be here to meet you at 2pm today.'

'What the hell for? I liked the other one for Christ's sake!' I was far too hung over for this bullshit today.

'For a boat trip,' she went on pleasantly, 'and don't be rude. Anyone in your position would be very pleased to get on a boat with him, trust me. It's leaving at the end of the week from somewhere in the South of France, not sure where yet. You'll spend two weeks sailing around the Côte d'Azur, stopping off at different places, and finally at the end of the trip, you'll anchor off the coast of Monaco and catch the Grand Prix. I understand Princess Diana's old chef will be cooking for you. The other bonus is you'll be allocated your own suite on board with your own bathroom too. How does it sound to you?'

She turned around to fetch some glasses from the cupboard. That gave me a chance to compose myself. Thank God! I couldn't give the game away, not just yet. Of course there was nothing I'd rather be doing than sunning myself on some yacht in the south of France, but just not with him! I had someone else on my mind….

'I'm supposed to be in Milan those two weeks. You know, doing some castings, building up some editorial and…'

She interrupted: 'Look my sweets; they say a career as a model is a short one, right? Well, a career like this one can be even shorter if you get my drift.'

'Career!' I blurted out almost choking, 'What fucking career?' This woman's a nut job.

She poured some wine and started to take a sip deliberately slowly. 'Blink and it's over,' she went on, 'There are very few people at the top of this tree and only one tree to climb. You're either in or you're out, it's really quite simple and anyway, there's no guarantee he will even take you.' She brushed the hair back from her face.

'Who the hell else is he going to take?' I asked sick of these silly arrangements already.

She paused before answering, helping herself to some nuts from a bowl on the table.

'Any of these girls,' she murmured, taking out what looked like a load of model index cards, and displaying them out over the table in front of me.

I cleared my throat and took a good look. There were some top notch girls among this lot that was for sure. I kept on flipping through, until I got to... *hang on a minute, it can't be, there's no way... what the he?* But there she was, clear as day, starring back at me in that oh so familiar pose of hers. Yes, I knew that chick anywhere, that really annoying face. How could I forget? I quickly reached over, grabbed Mimi's glass, and downed the still-chilled wine in one large gulp, I then pick up what remained of my glass and downed that too.

'What is it?' she asked. 'What's wrong? Slightly worried now?'

'Coke-head Kelly,' I replied, looking at the picture again, carefully this time. Yes I was sure. *Well, how about that?* 'She was evicted some months back from the agency apartment,' I told Mimi. 'Something about raiding the payphone system. I've not seen her since.'

'The payphone system?'

'It's a long story, one that I'm sure you don't want to hear now, but what that really means is she knows me well and I know her, and because of that we know all the same people and if she wanted to be an evil bitch, which she quite often is, she could quite easily blow my bubble as it were. It doesn't matter for her; half of London knows she's a full blown coke-head, but as for me, I've got more to lose, a lot more. What time are they arriving? The girls I mean.'

'Hum, right about now darling.' And with that the doorbell rang.

'Bugger', I swore, that was probably her. I jumped up and started darting around the kitchen. *What to do...* Mimi just sat there with that perverse smiles of hers glued to her lips. I swear, this twisted woman was actually enjoying this bullshit! I couldn't believe it. I quickly picked up my empty wine glass, the rest of the bottle and headed up the stairs to her bedroom, leaving her downstairs to conduct proceedings.

'What have I got myself into?' I muttered to myself on the way up the stairs. She came up behind me and slapped my arse on the way as she passed towards the front door.

'It will be fine,' she trilled, barely holding back her laughter. 'Trust me darling, leave it to me, everything will be fine.'

I had no idea what had happened in the kitchen while I was upstairs and I didn't really care, but after fifteen minutes or so the different pitches of female voices seemed to drift away and I was left with this rather deep, very-sure-of-itself male voice. But hang on a minute: that voice was getting nearer! In fact it was making its way up the stairs. *Why me?*

'Hello,' he called, 'Mimi's popped out to see the girls off. Why don't you come down and join me for a glass of wine. I've not got long.'

Christ, why the hell does she do that? I thought to myself, stepping down the stairs as slowly as possible. *Talk about being thrown in at the deep end!*

He was a very good looking man, tall, high cheekbones, jet black hair, milky skin, refined features, coal black eyes – and elegantly dressed in a black suit jacket and white shirt open at the neck. His eyes were piercing with a welcoming glint to them; however there was something about him I found totally unnerving.

We sat in total silence for what felt like far too long. He was studying me, watching me, waiting for me to break the ice. I wanted to know what he was thinking about, this weirdo, creepy, freak... - but then on second thoughts, perhaps I didn't.

Say something, I thought, but no sound would come out. I was stuck in a bubble of terrified silence. This was nothing like last's night at all: this was intense, too much to handle, not my thing at all and I began to feel desperately unprepared.

He could sense my nervousness and reached out to touch my hand, his fingertips grazing the tops of mine. I could feel the warmth from his hands. He was still gazing at me, not breaking eye contact, his right thigh pressed up against mine underneath the table. I started to panic: what was going on there?

Just as I thought the situation couldn't get any stranger I felt another person in the room with us. I quickly turned around. There was someone standing in the corner of the room. It couldn't be Mimi, could it? He said she had gone; how long had she been standing there? She must have let herself in really quietly through the back door. She was standing right inside the entrance, looking on intently.

Almost on cue my phone went off. I had a look at the caller ID. I recognized the international dialing code immediately. It was him, Money, he had come back to see me, just like he said he would and not as Mimi had told me. Thank fuck for that! But he wanted to see me now. This was going to be tricky; not only was I not in a position to leave right now but Money and I were not even supposed to have exchanged numbers.

I had broken the first rule of being employed by Mimi, if you can even call it that, employment! Everything had to go through her, even down to the simplest phone call. I had broken the rules and didn't I just know it. I started to shuffle uncomfortably in my chair, moving my hand away from Cartoon's and trying to disengage from the situation, when he called again. Money was more persistent this time, leaving what looked like message after message. I knew that if I didn't pick up soon, I would blow the whole thing. He had just flown half way across Europe to see me and here I was, in the kitchen of a lady who would probably sell her own children, if she had any, for less than the price of an average camel these days. I was quite sure, underneath it all, she had no loyalty to me, him or the next damned fool that blindly stumbled into the clutches of such a coldly clinical operation. I wanted out of this one, and I wanted out now.

Monday afternoon, Hyde Park Corner, London.

Three months later and we were in a large, expensive-looking suite in the Hilton Hotel, Park Lane, Mimi, Money and me.

He had arrived first and waited. Mimi and I arrived together after walking up from Hyde Park Corner. He had ordered a bottle of very expensive champagne which was left unopened in the bucket by the window.

Mimi sat in the middle of the sofa, looking firm but relaxed, controlling the pace of proceedings.

I was not far from her, but on the other side of the coffee table, in a stiff expensive-looking, velvet-lined chair, feeling distinctly out of my depth. I was, though, slightly comforted by the knowledge that this meeting could change everything. I could potentially be free to do as I pleased after this... well, for a time anyway.

What had seemed like a perfectly innocent arrangement just a few weeks ago had now turned into something altogether different. Mimi was not going to give me up without a fight. She fixed me with that steely stare of hers, ready go into battle and command her price. It was the money that got me into this horrendous arrangement in the first place and it was to be Money that would get me out. A lot of money. Money knew it. He got up from his chair not far from the window and looked out. From here we had a view over Hyde Park, Park Lane, and the surrounding buildings. Because it was the middle of the day there were not many people about and the constant stream of mid-week traffic was not half as ferocious as later on.

Money finally came over to join us, but didn't take a seat, preferring to stand mid-way between our chairs and a large glass coffee table. He bent down and removed a small black leather briefcase from underneath the table. Before Mimi had a chance to start negotiating, he walked over to the desk, opened the top right hand drawer and removed a long thin white envelope where the suitcase was laying. He opened the case just a crack, leaving only just enough room to remove what looked like a lot of £50 notes. He placed the flat, crisp notes into the white envelope and sealed it, handing it to Mimi.

'Thank you.' she said, feeling the thickness of the envelope against her fingertips, judging my worth in the palms of her hands. And that was it, it was done. He'd paid her to go away. *Wow, how cool!* I thought to myself; *wish I could pay people to go away, what a touch!*

There was a large marble bathroom leading off the main bedroom of the suite just to the right of me and I made a dash to it, almost on autopilot, closing the door firmly behind me before steadying myself on the washbasin. My throat was tight and I was finding it hard to catch my breath. I turned on the cold tap and started to splash water onto my face and chest, undoing my blouse, looking up to a catch a glimpse of my reflection in the mirror. Beads of sweat had started to appear on my chest and then I heard the main door of the suite close. She must have left. Thank fuck for that!

Then his arms were on either side of the washbasin and I could feel the warmth of his chest against me. I met Money's eyes in the mirror - they were sparkling with joy.

I reached out to stroke his face, he moved in closely to me, kissing me on the mouth and brushing my hair back from my cheekbones. He wasn't pushy and stood waiting for me to respond to him. However, I didn't want to do that, to give him the impression that I wanted a relationship with him. No way, José, not on your nelly!

I walked over to the window of the living room and opened up the bottle of champagne from earlier. There was still ice in the bucket and the bottle was still chilled. I poured us both a glass and handed one to him. His hand was shaking too as he took it. We both drank in virtual silence, apart from the noise of the traffic drifting through the now-open window.

I started wondering why and how it ever got so complicated. *It was all about the money surely!*

The Pub, West London.

Seven in the evening the day after Mimi and the money business, I went to the Earl Percy, a pub on Ladbroke Grove. I had not heard from Money since leaving the hotel, probably for the best as I still hadn't fully processed the last 24 hours. So I went back to my usual pastime of hanging out at the pub. I needed to take my mind off things for a while and drinking usually did that - until I sobered up anyway.

For these excursions I usually had two partners in crime: Darkstar, 5' 10", slim, attractive, highly entertaining but highly unemployable. The main thing Dark and I had in common was our love of drinking and our ability to get sacked from almost every London model agency within a 10 mile radius.

The other was my 'on again off again', part-time musician lunatic boyfriend, Rebelstar. Like all second rate musicians he was sometimes homeless and most times penniless, just as Mimi divined. He'd spend most of his days writing poetry, banging musical instruments or banging older women for money as girls like me weren't dumb enough to pay for him on a regular basis.

On an irregular basis, I'd take him to the pub for a few. Darkstar would invite herself along and she'd spend the evening trying to find some bloke to buy her drinks, usually an older bloke. We'd stay there until we were completely pissed, then pop around to the house of some feckless French aristocrat in Holland Park, on the off chance that his mother might be away, that's when he would sometimes have something we could sniff.

On this occasion, we never made it to Holland Park as the all-important phone call I'd been expecting all day was just about to stop me in my tracks.

It wasn't that I didn't want to hear from Money, I just didn't know exactly what to do with the man, and he definitely did know what to do with me! I finally answered after leaving my phone on the bar for quite a few rings. I let him speak first, trying to read the tone in his voice. 'Hey Kid,' he said hesitantly. 'Are you there?'

'Yes, I'm here' I said, starting feeling distinctly uncomfortable so took the phone outside.

'Look, I've been thinking. A lot has happened in the past few weeks and the best thing to do would be for us to go away for a week or so, you know, get some sun, what do you think?' He paused. 'I mean, what would you like to do? Do you have anywhere in mind?'

I replied without hesitation: 'I know exactly what we'll do', I said clearing my throat whilst rubbing my hands together. 'We shall go to the south of France. Tonight.' I added. 'Let's leave tonight!'

A long silence came on the other end of the line. I don't know if it were shock, a disturbance or something else but he finally responded with 'I'll book the flights then' and that's exactly what we did.

Chapter 4

Written whilst listening to 'Hold my Hand' by Hootie and the Blowfish

•

Still June 1996, 12 noon, Private Airfield, England.

What used to be regarded as a stressful and tiresome experience, for me anyway, had now been changed to one of pure pleasure and delight, I thought to myself, as I took a step back to admire the platinum tones in the aircraft. Mmhmm.

The only thing I was able to compare it to, due to my lack of informative life experiences, would be the sleek exterior of an expensive car. So perfectly crafted I was almost afraid to touch it and that was just the outside.

The interior, well, that would leave even the more sophisticated among us feeling inferior: muted tones, aesthetically pleasing curves and translucent partitions made this private jet more unique than some. But the real joy of these carefully crafted machines were the hidden extra's, as in champagne on tap, so pass me a glass and I'll tell you the rest, slipping my shoes off in the process…

But just to recap: I was just about to get on a plane, owned by who knows who, flying who knows where, for who knows what. But it was an option all the same. An option I intended to take. And with that I leaned over the front seat to instruct the pilots (there were two of them) that I was indeed ready to commit to this perilous journey. I then fastened my seat belt and leaned over to check on Darkstar and Rebelstar who were sitting in the only two other passenger seats.

Well, you didn't honestly think I'd come on my own, did you? I really didn't know just how foolish this decision was about to become but now, looking back with hindsight I suppose it was inevitable… I cracked open the Bollinger and poured myself and the other two reprobates the largest glass I could find of what I considered at the time to be the only medicinal substance on the planet. It slid down our throats faster than Laurence of Arabia could have looked for water in the desert, as did the next, and the next. The valium helped too as we were now well on our way to the land of the weak and road of the wicked. No going back. It was too late for that.

'Hey babe, come on', came the bellowing voice directly into my left ear drum, 'we are here sweetness, this is It.' and sure enough he was right. We'd landed. Rebel unbuckled the belt from around my waist and I felt a lightening of tension that all but disappeared as my head pounded with the pain of dehydration that only should happen, well, to this extent, no more than twice in any normal person's lifetime.

It took me a while to come round too. The mind willing but body in a dreadful state of disrepair. *How did it come to this?* I thought despairingly as I caught a glimpse of my reflection in one of the windows. Who the hell can go from looking reasonably well to looking like a complete train wreck in only a matter of hours? Well, me for a start, obviously!

Flanked by Rebel and Darkstar who, incidentally, were in no finer state than I, we exited the plane placing a shaky toe onto probably the most expensive landing soil in the world.

I glanced over at Darkstar as she drained the remaining champers from the bottle then lunged over to me planting a big fat kiss on my neck; this is nothing new for Dark as her preference had always been women as opposed to men when it came to sexual orientation.

'Are you going to bonk him?' she asked with an enigmatic grin, glancing over at Rebel trying to read the emotion on his face. I turned away from them. *Of course I'm not going to!* I thought to myself, *It's all about the money* I reminded myself with a silly smile.

We all picked up our various weekend holdalls; mine a Vuitton, a prezzie, no less from Money. Some days previously. We start walking away from the plane and towards the customs house, the silence punctuated only by our footsteps on the tarmac.

'Well if you do bonk him', Dark went on, following behind me in the shadow of my footsteps, as Rebel was too, 'make sure I'm there to watch'.

'Yes, me too' added Rebel, draining the last from his glass and handing it back to one of the pilots and with that a perpetual form of laughter filled the air. We were all too aware I suppose of the perverse nature of the arrangement.

There was no time in my mind to question details like this, we were here now and I for one would make damn sure we'd make the most of it, with finances as perilous as my own, who knew where the next holiday was coming from.

So, with that thought, I reached into my back pocket, to remove my last Xanax tablet from its foil casing, popped it into my mouth and waited for the world to turn into a happy place once more; everything was going to be fine then, wasn't it? Nothing but clear blue skies and a blue green ocean to think about... *this is the life...* I thought to myself, *this is the new little life...*

The sun brought with it a warmth and intensity of light I'd not witnessed before, even on the continent. We were standing facing the Carlton Intercontinental, one of the world's most photographed hotels.

Like the rest of Cannes, it looked as if it had just recently undergone a face lift - the hotel that is – however, I could just as easily be describing the people to think of it.

'Look at its twin cupolas,' remarked Rebel standing to the left of me, looking up, 'I hear they were erected in 1912 and were modeled on the breasts of the courtesan La Belle Otero.' he added with a smile. We both exchanged quizzical glances, and then looked on together. 'How quaint,' I finally remarked, never ceasing to be amazed by the randomness of Rebel's occasional knowledge and his fluid observations on useless subjects.

'Anything else I need to know before we check in?' I remarked as we mounted the steps to the entrance lobby. But before I could finish my sentence I felt a light tap on my left shoulder 'Hello there Kid' came the deep familiar man's voice, it was Money. 'I've been expecting you' and with that he kisses me lightly on both cheeks.

I realized that I'd missed looking into his kind dark eyes, whilst smelling his wallet. He looks relaxed, tanned and slightly plumper than I remembered him; he was my Money, with the wallet of course which I felt a gravitational pull towards each time we met. 'And I see you've brought some friends with you' he added, making a gesture towards Rebel and Dark.

'Oh yes,' I said clearing my throat uncomfortably, 'first time on a private plane and all that, moral support you see?' 'Well', he remarked, sounding thoroughly unconvinced that they should have been there, 'As you wish'. And with that he got the porter to show us to our respective rooms. But where was he staying?

Rebel and Dark were to share a small junior suite on the third floor, booked last minute by the very generous Money. It looked out onto La Croisette which was the Riviera's so called classiest promenade.

I on the other hand would be on the fourth floor royal suite, way too big for one person but utterly elegant all the same. At the foot of my room were double French doors that opened up to look over a private beach, not bad.

If you looked north east along the dazzling white sandy coast line you'd find the beautiful but little Antibes, nuzzling next to Vallauris and Golfe Juan (Picasso territory) so Rebel reliably informed me. Moving down slightly further and you would, at some point, be able to bathe yourself in the intense coloured light of Matisse's Chappelle du Rosaire in Vence.

However I myself was more interested in the lump of red porphyritic rock known as the Massif de l'Esterel. Something about it captivated me: it rested at the foot of St-Raphael, a beachside resort town a couple of kilometers southeast of roman Fréjus, but something in my mind began to remind me that we were in fact not there to be intrepid explorers, and Money had some very different plans for us, or should I say me anyway.

He had some very different plans for me but what did I expect…

nothing for nothing in this world I s'pose and anyway, I could do a lot worse than Money I'm sure.

Sunshine spilled into the room via the open French doors leading out onto the beach, renewing my sense of wellbeing. It was impossible to dislike this place if you had any sense of magic or imagination about you. My persistent feelings of the blues (it happens sometimes) weren't hard to shift this morning as I watched Money sleeping motionless beside me.

I slowly started to drift off again into a dreamlike sleep when I was abruptly awoken by someone tap tapping at the door, breaking the silence of the dawn and the stillness of the morning. I slowly got up to answer, being mindful not to wake Money, as a rare moment of philosophical intimacy - or any kind of intimacy - was not on the cards this morning, or any morning for that matter.

I grabbed a long white fluffy bath robe from behind the door and draped it around my naked frame, enjoying the softness of the cotton against my skin, I then opened the door. 'Morning Miss' came the soft French accent of the young room service porter, his gaze lingering ever so slightly too long on my chest which was peeking out of my gapingly large robe as I took the breakfast tray from him and placed it gently down on a Victorian style chair somewhere near the foot of the bed.

I then reached over to Money's side of the room and picked up his deep brown Hermes wallet, the one I missed the smell of, which was resting on a small rosewood bed side table, one of many ornate pieces of furniture residing in the room. I tipped the porter as I grabbed the note from the breakfast tray that I incidentally didn't order. 'Merci Madame' as he accepted the euros and swiftly closed the door, not before having a quick glance towards the bed in an overly curious manner. *The cheek of the French!* I thought to myself as I settled down to read the note that had been left on the tray next to the unopened bottle of champagne. Who could this be from?

'Dear Miss Thing' it read, 'We hope you enjoyed your night of passion last night however we, unfortunately, got held up at the hotel bar and where unable to make it up to your suite for viewing – not to worry as there's a speed boat booked for us later today in anticipation of a beach party taking place at the Val Rouge – 20 mn by sea we were told. Dress for success, as in hardly any clothes at all and make sure you bring Money as he's paying. Lots of love, and our condolences for last night'. Signed: Rebel and Darkstar x.

The boat in question turned out to be a 1.2million 1, 350 hp Mercedes-Benz cigarette speed boat.

'How the fuck did you find this?' I questioned Rebel as he slid his right hand down the hull of the super beast of a machine emphasizing to me the sleekness of the design.

'Well,' he went on, 'after a few too many in the hotel bar last night, I decided to take a stroll down to the marina - where we are now in fact, right on this very spot - when I spied I man rolling a special cigarette, you know the kind I like?'

'Oh, right,' I replied, 'the herb variety?'

'Yes that's the one.' he went on, 'Anyway, I quite fancied a toke on this thing so I decided to make friends with the guy, you know, out of politeness and all that.'

'Oh, of course', I responded, observing to myself that Rebel always seemed to find a degree of politeness when it benefited him the most, 'OK, go on', I said, allowing him to finish the story.

'Well, so, this bloke and I started talking, you know, about the world and stuff, best place to grow herbs and...'

'Yes, I get the picture,' I interrupted, 'what happened then?'

'Well then Dark rocked up, champagned up to the eye balls from the bar - fuck knows who paid for the drinks incidentally - anyway she then starts talking to the guy too, telling him how fond she was of fast boats, champagne and particularly French men, as he was, French I mean.'

'But she doesn't even like men?' I piped up, finding this story anything but as amusing as he clearly thought it was.

Rebel ignored this comment and went back to the story: 'So anyway,' he went on, 'then the guy told us that if we found someone to rent the boat tomorrow, which is now today...'

'Yes, yes, I get that' I interjected again, slightly irritated by the whole thing by this point.

'He would take us to the best party on the Riviera', Rebel went on excitedly, 'Well come on babe', he reached out to grab my arm, 'How could I say no and anyway, it'll lessen the pressure off you, you know with Money and all that. This is right up his pie hole, he'll be so distracted by all the beautiful women at the place, he won't even know we're there or not there as the case maybe. In fact he won't know which direction to turn fast enough, with all that flesh on display. Then you, I and Dark can finally let loose and have some fun! Come on... just trust me on this one, will you?'

Well, it sounded like a plan but one thing I'd learnt from years of dealings with Rebel was to never be too shocked or amazed at what was just about to happen next, and I don't necessarily mean in a good way either! The other point he was failing to notice was the fact I wanted to spend time with Money....find out exactly what this guy was worth and all that. My last minute decision to bring him and Dark had been a severe error of judgment on my part, but too late for regrets now.

I sat down on the edge of the jetty, allowing my toes to gently graze the surface of the twinkling blue water, a warm wet hit of sensory pleasure. It felt good, I closed my eyes, my awareness telling me this quite possibility could be the only enjoyable part to the day I had in store.

Why did he want me here anyway? Money that was. What could I possibly bring to his life that he couldn't find elsewhere? Or buy elsewhere should I say. As for me, well, I at this point only saw my options as limited, I mean, what were the choices? I could die, end up in the loony bin, or get on this boat with these cats...

After 30 seconds of careful consideration, 'I'll think I'll try the boat' and with that I collected my thoughts well enough to tolerate the day ahead. *It won't be that bad* I told myself, popping another Zanex, *I'll get through it*.

I looked up to find Rebel animatedly guiding two people down the jetty from the marina. I took a closer look, just as I thought; it was Darkstar and Money looking happy and relaxed as they strolled along together in the midday heat, Dark looking something like an extra from Baywatch and Money resembling a Middle Eastern version of a Ralph Lauren ad, if this is at all imaginable. A match made in hell if you ask what I think, but who was asking me about anything come to think of it. My opinion just didn't count for anything these days, if it ever had at all. All I had to do was show up and things just happened and anyway, it was all about the money I reassured myself *keep your eyes on the money and prepare for the boat.*

My legs where shaking as I boarded the boat. I was not sure if it were nerves or the company (of some unknown French man, Rebel and Dark), or the speed of the boat that I was unsure of but at any rate I felt uneasy. Dark and Rebelstar where already two sheets to the wind (intoxicated and unsteady). How they managed that I didn't know, as it was barely midday. Money appeared not to notice however, and the French man seemed oblivious to any form of social interaction that didn't involve Money, so that counted us out. In fact, I was quite sure he'd sell his mother for the right price, as the only thing or person he seemed to give any notice to would be Money and his bulging wallet; that was my job surely! But we pressed on regardless.

I couldn't tell you exactly how long it took us to reach the Pamplona beach in St Tropez, but it can't have been any longer than 30 minutes traveling at speed. I'd prefer not to recount to you but let's just say the thought of death was imminent.

The beach party that we were about to attend went under the name of 'le voile rouge', a sanctuary for the French aristocracy from what I could gather, designed for the underdeveloped mind and the overdeveloped wallet. A place where they'd quite happily sit your grandmother next to a girl partially naked, having Chandon sipped from her belly button, but that's the French for you.

At the front would be the main French restaurant, which was nothing worth shouting about, in fact slightly passé as it seemed to attract routine orientated Americans trying desperately to behave like the big shots they weren't. This led out into an open bar.

Now, this was when the fun really started as the place was cramped full of billionaires driving Bugatti's and women whose sole ambitions in life would be to do all the things that they shouldn't really be doing. I know this sounds slightly familiar but anyway… here we were… we had arrived to what must have been one of the most seductive views in town….the glowing terracotta roofs and a church tower complete with distinctive Provencal campanile.

The faint throbbing of euro trash music became apparent as we slowed the speed right down and let the boat naturally drift onto the beach. A few locals jumped down from their sun loungers to help us, Money threw them a rope, and one of the men waded slightly into the water, took the rope from us and secured it to the nearest safe place. Money jumped out the boat first, only just getting his feet wet, followed by myself, Dark and Rebel's. As my feet touched the soil, a strange sense of euphoria began to flood my body.

Money had one of the staff from the restaurant come down the beach with a tray full of drinks - they obviously knew we were coming. I took a drink from the tray thanking the lady as did Money, and we began to stroll up the beach together, his arm slipped around my un-waif like sized hips. Rebel and Darkstar in hot pursuit not far behind.

I didn't know whether it was the warmth of the sun on my skin, the lapping of the sea beneath my feet or the atmosphere of the beach that did it, but something began to feel natural about the whole thing, my resentment of being there flooding away in an instant. In fact, the why's and how's of how we met drifted away like the tide of the sea and the changing of the seasons. What was it about the money?...

The table they found was laced with rose petals and the air hung with the sweet smell of honey nectar and lily. He took me in his arms pulling me towards him, our bodies met. He touched my lips tenderly; I moved in to meet his lips, closing my eyes as he kissed my mouth. It started to feel strangely intimate and I moved away, more startled by my own behaviour than his, I mean, this wasn't part of the plan...

The table was set for four and we all took a seat, me next to Money, Rebel and Dark beside each other. The waitress made her way back to the table 'Can I get anyone anything else to drink?' she asked her eyes fixed on me the whole time, I had no idea why. 'Yes', responded Money, not even bothering to look at the drinks menu, 'We'll have two bottles of Cristal, one on ice and anything else these guys would like to add' he added, gesturing towards Dark and Rebelstar.

Bad move, I thought to myself, any more alcohol so soon in the day and it was an afternoon destined for destruction, no questions. Who was I to point out the obvious, I was just here to look pretty and with that I encouraged Money to give the champagne a try. This took less persuasion than it usually would (he hardly was a big drinker). He lifted his glass to his lips and started to sip in a playful manner, his other arm lightly tapping the underneath side of his chair to the rhythm of the music. This was a good sign, I thought to myself.

I, Dark and Rebel however had completely different ideas as to what constituted a good time and the hour was still young.

We all picked up our respective glasses; 'A toast I think is in order' chimed in Rebelstar, with a wink of the eye in my direction and a forward motion gesture with the arms like something out of Star Trek in our direction.

Oh fuck! What the hell is he going to say! Rebel and I had some unresolved sexual history, a really disastrous relationship in other words, and seeing me there with Money, even if only momentarily, was enough of a catalyst to set him off, especially after a few, as he had had.

Dark being Dark was addicted to the drama of it all and did

nothing in attempt to play down his public displays of ridiculousness if and when they happened. However, I felt pretty secure in the fact he wouldn't kick off here, not in front of all these people, surely!

He (Rebel) then held the table with one hand for support and, with the other less supportive hand, downed the drink fresh from the bottle. I had no idea exactly which champagne it was, but let's just say it was a very expensive mouthful.

Dark, adding to proceedings, trotted around to the other side of the table, straight past the champagne (how out of character!) and straight for a redundant looking microphone. After a little pirouette, she delicately picked up the mic, giving it a tap to make sure it was on. And it was…

'Oh groovy' she announced, jutting her weight onto one hip and waiting for the kind of response from people that only someone like Dark can command.

Rebel had now risen to his feet too, and was doing some mock rave dance at the table. 'Yeah babe', he addressed Dark, 'Let's get this show on the woawd!' and with that, he whipped off his top, exposing the kind of torso most men dream of and most women dream about.

But before Dark had even reached him back at the table, another pair of hands had come into action and they certainly weren't mine or Dark's. These were the keen fingers of an older and very distinguished lady, who by now was sitting right next to him, reaching up and attempting to pour champagne onto his naked torso. And he had the nerve to complain about my behaviour in public?

Money looked back at me and I back at Money, no words were spoken between us. I topped up our glasses of champagne and started to drink in a last ditch attempt to drown out my remaining consciousness.

Dark by this point had picked up her own new group of admirers, stripped down to a tiny pink bikini, and had lead them back to our table, most of them are half naked, intoxicated and up for anything...

I took a closer look at the lady swilling champagne in an up close and personal manner, within close proximity to Rebelstar's gyrating groin... *Oh fuck it's not?* I said to myself, downing another glass of Cristal that *looks suspiciously like Zsa Zsa Gabor*. Money now started to look away as two men began to spray Darkstar with champagne in close proximity to the table, one from the front and one from behind.

I was so wet from the residue of the champers that it had soaked through my dress, which incidentally was white, and we all know what that meant. Within moments I started to look like an extra in a soft sore porn movie as my dress was so see through I might as well have worn nothing at all.

I felt a hand on my back, starting to rub it affectionately. Assuming it was Money I allowed it to continue, whatever it took to get through this and all that. I started to muse until I heard a low French man's voice. 'Oh no!' realizing it was not Money at all but some random stranger getting close up and personal with me! I took a second look, only to see a wealth of information throbbing through the silhouette of his trousers.

'Christ!' I tried and maneuver myself away from him but it was no use and there was nowhere to run. Where the fuck was Money! I stood up to get a better view of the restaurant area and spied him out of the corner of my eye. *Crap, I think he's leaving,* 'Money!' I shouted, 'Money!!!' I was screaming at the top of my lungs. But it was no use.

'I am a Barbie girl, in a Barbie world' was now being pumped at full volume out of every possible speaker, there was no way he was going to hear. The French man now had me in both arms, echoing the lyrics to the fucking synthetic music 'I feel plastique' he sang, 'it's fantastique!'

That was it. I had just about had enough. I propelled myself up onto the table, my champagne soaked body sliding across the length of it with ease, the French man in hot pursuit. 'Hey!' he yelled, 'Don't leave me so soon, my sweetie, my angel, my dahrling!' Champagne glasses were flying as my feet reached the other side of the floor. Luckily, all the other party goers were so inebriated (Rebel and Dark included), no one seemed to notice the mayhem that was going on around them...

I felt a hand reach out and grab my arse. Grabbing the hand, both arms behind me, I spun around to face him 'Look you dump French fuck' I yelled, beyond reasoning at this point, ' I've had enough!' and with that gave him what I thought was a gentle push back. He stumbled and fell into two helpless waiters who happened to be standing there, which gave me just enough time to run down to the shore line.

Money was there, instructing the money hungry French man that had brought us that he was wanting to leave the party this instant, on his own. I was out of breath by then but kept on running. Money stood waiting as the French man cast the ropes off in preparation to get the boat in the water. 'Money!' I yelled again, in one last vain attempt to get his attention but to no use. He was starring reflectively out to sea, lost in the thoughts of his own world, untouchable.

I stopped for a second in a reflective moment. Why was I running like this? I clutched my panting chest, overwhelmed. My legs began to give way and I found myself sitting on the sand, head in hands, and salty hard tears of emotion swelling up in my eyes. But for what? I didn't even like this guy... I didn't need him, or his stupid boat... yes, that's right... I was going to make much more money than Money ever had, I'd buy his silly boat and blow it up... I'd show him! Now... where the hell were those cig's of mine... as I watched the boat gently bob out to sea...

Chapter 5

Written whilst listening to 'One more chance' by B.I.G.

July 1996, The Pub, Ladbroke Grove, London.

It was a grim and rainy day. I was down to my last two Marlboro Lights and the only money I had on me was of the change variety. I had no will or inclination to do anything other than nurse the drink on the table in front of me. Then the next. And the next.

So, what was the good news? Well, there wasn't any good news. I had been back well over a week now and nothing from Money, not that I really wanted him to contact me, but it was something to do.

My agency were seething as I hadn't really informed them of my little plan to go the south of France and, subsequently, made them look stupid when I didn't show up for things but tell me something that I don't know.

Rebel and Dark unfortunately made it back to the UK in one piece and had now gone back to their usual bullshit routines of bad behaviour. Needless to say, the pair of them didn't give a shit about the emotional consequences of our trip, or the mental wellbeing of anyone other than their little tiny selves, which brought me on to that other form of witchcraft which was Mimi. I had neither heard from her, nor seen her. Probably for the best, I was sure.

So, just to put everything into perspective, I had no more future plans other than to forget what had happened the last time I tried to make some plans which, as we all know, went badly wrong.

Talking about wrong, why in heavens' name was my glass empty? I trotted over to the bar to refill and attempted to work out who the next poor bastard was that Darkstar had lined up to buy us drinks all night. It had to be one of these guys here; I had a look along the length of the bar.

Wait a minute, that looked suspiciously like that other reprobate I knew, and sure enough it was: Rebel relaying a story to some unsuspecting tourists about his connections to the British Ministry of Defense, of all things. *Where did he dream this bullshit from?* I thought to myself, accepting a drink refill from Dark and finding ourselves the quietest darkest table in the corner of the pub, in the Earl Percy to be precise.

Dark then went forth to open her mouth, attempting some form of conversation I gather. However, I was just not able for it today. I reached across the table and gently placed my left hand over her mouth.

'Please,' I asked her, 'not today. Let's just sit here quietly and enjoy each other's company, in silence, shall we?' I closed my eyes in mock meditation...

'But, hang on a minute', she went on, 'If I were not allowed to speak and we were to sit here, you with your eyes closed, I could quite easily not be here?' she questioned.

I gave her a look as if to say 'Well I didn't like to say', to reiterate the point that I was just not pleased with her after everything that had happened. However, it didn't really take Einstein to work that one out.

'As you wish' she retorted in a mock Arabian accent, reminiscent of Money, naturally.

We both sat there in silence after that last comment, I didn't know whether to laugh or hit her at this point.

I then started to feel a dark presence looming over me, someone standing to the right of me. I looked up, 'Oh, it's you,' I said, giving Rebel a light peck on the cheek, not that he deserved it of course, but I welcomed the distraction from my own thoughts anyway.

'Did you miss me?' he asked, bending down slightly to look in my face. 'Like a continuous headache' I replied in all seriousness, as that was exactly what he was to me.

He sat down in the chair next to mine looking very pleased with himself, but I just couldn't be asked to ask him what all the extra smugness was about. It was bound to be something morally wrong at any rate.

'So look', he went on, reaching under the table and pulling out a bottle of Jack Daniels that you could bet your life on was certainly not purchased from the premises - not that I gave a damn, I just didn't want to be kicked out just yet - it was cold outside and I knew these shorts were a bad idea... but anyway, I made myself comfortable on the seat next to him, waiting for the bullshit to start. *What has he dreamt up this month*, I thought to myself, *only time will tell...*

He produced three shot glasses, obviously stolen from the bar. He started to decant some of the JD which he was now balancing between his knees so not to be seen, into the three glasses.

'So look,' he began, handing us the glasses, 'I'd like to share some news with you' he said, touching me by the arm in an overly convincing manor.

'Oh yes' I said, skeptically taking the shot of JD and downing it in one. *God! It tastes foul, why do I do this to myself?* I had never been one for spirits, but it certainly brought some warmth to my cold tired chest. They both followed suit and we were again momentarily united in one common pleasure.

'So yes,' he went on, 'I meet this bloke the other day who said he knew Kimmi, you remember Kimmi, right?' Dark and I looked at each other blankly.

'No, can't say we do' Dark retorted.

'KIMMI' Rebel reiterated, 'come on, there was only one Kimmi!' He swept his glass off the table and took another shot.

Just at that moment, I remembered: 'Oh God!' I exclaimed, half out loud and half to myself, 'How could I forget!', or anyone forget for that matter. What a girl! Or woman should I say, as this was a few years back when we first met and she was in her late 20s then, not that age meant anything when it came to a creature like that, I mean, that was a special brain on that one...

Kimmi was beautiful, there was no two ways about that, but she used her beauty for all the wrong things, with the mind of a criminal. Yeah, the chick was dangerous, with the body of a stripper... well; she was a stripper... and the rest...

It was Dark's turn to talk now, having stayed suspiciously silent since the Kimmi subject came up. 'Didn't she meet some banker or something? Worked in the city?'

'Go on, make me laugh', I interrupted, 'she's turned her life around and now she's a Christian?'

Dark and I both laughed in unison. This was usually the point in the day when we'd take the person that we'd been discussing and make up lewd and obscene stories, probably because it helped us forget about our own petty lives. It whiled away the time anyway.

But Rebel stopped us dead there 'You two may mock, but Miss Kimmi has done pretty well for herself, that's for sure' – there was a long pause.

'Apparently' chipped in Dark, still completely unconvinced and as dry and sardonic as ever.

'Ok' went on Rebelstar, clearing his throat and getting back into his story telling stride. He reached down under the table, located the Jack Daniels bottle balanced between his legs once more and started to top up our shot glasses: one, first for myself, two, then Dark's, three, then his own.

'Anyway, so the other day,' he went on, 'I was strolling back from a party in Holland Park. It had been all-nighters, I was pretty wrecked in fact and I just couldn't face breakfast in the café, you know two poached eggs on brown toa...'

Dark finished his sentence 'toast with just one rasher of very streaked bacon, yes we know'.

'Ok yes, that's right.' he went back to the story, 'so anyway, I decided instead to knock back a Bloody Mary, hair of the dog and all that, but I just couldn't face the social interaction of the pub for this ritual. So, I popped into the 5th floor bar of Harvey Nicks, Kimmi's old hangout, and while I was there I bumped into Chloe, Kimmi's old bestie and loyal side kick, you remember Chloe, right?'

'Vaguely' I replied, looking at Dark,

'Not really' she replied, looking back at me.

'Well, anyway,' said Rebel 'it's unimportant. But what was important was what she told me about Kimmi.'

'Oh, go on!' I said with renewed interest.

'Miss Kimmi is now living the high life in New York, 5th Avenue princess apparently! Chloe had just got back from visiting her there, in this beautifully big apartment overlooking Central Park. They dined in The Plaza for breakfast; Macy's for lunch and mingled with that cream of New York society come the evening time. She's got it made babe!' he said, looking at me.

I slammed my shot glass down on the table, demanding another. Sometimes other people's successes were harder to swallow than a hardcore shot of whisky on an empty stomach.

I downed it in one, still swallowing hard - not the first time in my life - so I went on, still feeling the sting of this information: 'What does this wonderful news have to do with me?'

'Well,' went on Rebel enthusiastically, 'she's lonely out there. Banker wanker is at work all day long and there are only so many times you can go around lower east side art galleries on your own.' *As if she goes to art galleries,* I thought to myself. Anyway, he went on: 'Of course they aren't married and all of the other bankers' wives don't like the look of Kimmi, so she's forever being excluded from their gatherings. So, anyway, Kimmi needed something to do with her days as Banker asked her to cut her hours at The Hustler Club down to weekends.'

He took a small sip of whisky, just to wet his lips, 'and now she's taken an unpaid position (no experience no money) at an up and coming New York model agency, booking the girls and stuff. She's loving it apparently and that's when she thought of you!'

'What about me?' I questioned apprehensively.

'She wants you to fly out there; she's got work for you, good stuff too!'

'Good stuff to Kimmi usually involves taking your kit off' remarked Dark. Rebel made no comment.

There was a long uncomfortable silence. She was right of course, Dark that is, but that was the least of my concerns right now. I wanted to get off there badly and away from this shit hole. *Anything but this,* I thought to myself.

I took a sigh. 'It's tempting,' I said, 'but if I do that my agency here will sack me, on the spot'.

'Fuck them' said Rebel. Dark agreed. 'All they've done for you is be on your back for the last few weeks and as for their apartment, it's a joke compared to this' as he whipped out a folded photograph from his jacket pocket. '62nd and Broadway', he announced, 'Columbus Circle babe, this is where you'd be staying in New York, this is THEIR agency apartment'. I leaned over and took a look, as did Dark.

I got a tingle down my spine... Wowser, it was beautiful, I had to admit, but how was I going to do this? My portfolio was fine, but no agency was going to fund my trip over there, having not seen me first, it just didn't happen like that.

'How am I supposed to get there?' I asked Rebel, knowing that if I were to rely on his organizational skills it would be shady to say the least.

'Well you know the Banker,' he went on,

'Oh what, her Banker?' I replied.

'Yes', he said, 'her Banker, let's call him Bill for sake of argument. Banker Bill would like to sponsor your trip out there in return for you posing as his girlfriend at corporate events.'

'But I thought that was Kimmi's job?' I said, confused now.

'No, no, no, babe', interrupted Dark, 'this is how it works: girls like Kimmi are for, you know, mmhmm...' she looked to Rebelstar for some help, 'for behind closed doors' replied Rebel 'you know, not for public display. But you, on the other hand,' he stopped. Dark finished his sentence 'you would be going to represent English, you know, make him look good and stuff.' 'What do you think?' he asked looking encouraging.

I looked to Dark before answering. *As if she's got the answers,* I think to myself, *God I must be in a bad way if it's come to this...* the whole thing was confusing and would never work, not that I really cared too much at that point.

'Well I think you should go babe' Dark finally said, 'I mean, what have you got to lose?' she added gesturing around her.

She had more than a point, I mused, and if things went badly wrong I could always come back, I mean, it's not as if things had gone really right for me here anyway, I was sacrificing nothing really.

I got up from the table feeling distinctly light headed - hardly a surprise – 'I'll be back peeps.' I said, steadying myself slightly on the chair then heading in the direction of the door. I fumbled in my pocket for my ciggi's - second to last one - located a light, and popped outside the pub.

The air was light and still. It must have been just approaching early evening as dusk was setting in, the only time of the day to see London really. I could have smoked inside if I'd really wanted to but what would have been the point of that? I needed some space to think on my own, evaluate everything. New York had been calling me a while now, perhaps too long?

30000 feet up.

Dah dah dar di dar, dah dah dar di dah, start spreading the news, I'm leaving today, I wanna be a part of it, New York, New York! Oh yeah!

Ok that's enough for now. Better get sober, my flight touches down in approximately 25 minutes and I wanna be prepared to take in that mythical landscape that is N-Y-C, the land of stylish concrete and skyscrapers. I had no idea what time it would be when I landed and I didn't really care, as long as Kimmi was there to meet me at arrivals, it was all good with me...

So here I was, JFK baby! It was a little intimidating as far as airports went. In fact, that was so much of an understatement it was almost a lie as to me right now it seemed one of the maddest, baddest airports I had ever encountered.

It was big and busy with everyone on a mission, four runways, seven terminals and was as mental as NY itself. Luckily my luggage came through quickly and I sauntered through customs, no problem, now where the fuck was Kimmi? I needed to get out of here, quickly.

I looked around, surprised I couldn't see her. She was hardly the kind of chick you could miss: close to 6 foot, a mass of champagne bottle blonde hair, the boobies where real and difficult to miss, as was the rap video-esc way she walked. It may have sounded like a nightmare waiting to happen, I know, but add the prettiest baby doll face to the mix and you had a recipe for destruction, that was for sure.

Kimmi could get people to do things for her like I'd never known before… thank God she was not running the country! I thought as she rocked up, front entrance, in a pink Cadillac of all things. People had started to stop and stare already, rap music blaring, 'biggy, biggy, biggy, can't you see, sometimes your words just hypnotize me' I heard belt out as she crashed the breaks to a halt and flung open the passenger door.

'Hop in babe!' she yelled, paying absolutely no attention whatsoever to the big black suitcase I was holding. I wheeled it around to the back of the car, eventually managing to get it in ok, then walked around the side and let myself in the passenger's side of the car.

'Whoever this car belongs to Kimmi' I said, taking her arm as I reached across to give her a big kiss on the cheek, 'give it back to them!' and we both erupted with laughter.

She gave my body a tight squeeze in her arms 'Oooh, I missed you English, we're gonna have some fun together girlfriend' she said in a mock Britney spears accent.

'Yeah, I missed you too Kimmi.' I said. 'If there is anyone I can have fun with, it's definitely you!' I said laughing, and with that I lit up my last remaining ciggi.

We cranked up the music and zoomed off down the highway 'Biggy, biggy, biggy can't you see... sometimes your words just hypnotize me...'

I must have drifted off at some point in the journey as when I came to me we were somewhere completely unrecognizable. 'Upper West Side baby' Kimmi mused as I opened my eyes. We had driven up outside an apartment block not far from the Hudson River on one side and Central Park West on the other. The building in question was old school, grand and sophisticated, filled with aging liberals, retired actors and musicians at a guess but really, I had no clue who's home we were at or about to enter.

'This is Marti and my apartment' Kimmi said, gesturing up at the magnificent building, 'we're right at the top' she added, 'the penthouse honey child!' Oh God, she was back to the southern American drool, which she did quite well considering she was originally from British Colombia, Canada, no less.

So, I was beginning to wake properly now. 'Who the hell is Marti?' I asked, just about managing to get the question out, God I felt rough! Must be hit by jet lag or something. 'The banker babe, remember, the one I live with, the one that paid for your flight, business class right?', 'Oh yeah, right' I answered, completely forgetting that I actually got here courtesy of someone else.

'So you wanna meet him right?' she added,

'Well yeah Kimmi' I answered, 'but preferably not right now if that's ok, need to chill first you know, relax a bit.'

'Yeah, yeah, no sweat princess, he's not finishing work till 8pm and not home till 9, so that gives us a chance to relax and kick back. I'll fill you in on the agency too; it's about a 20min drive to the agency apartment from here so let's wait until tomorrow for that, they're not expecting you till then anyway. Ok peeps?' she added, rubbing my shoulder.

'Ok boss' I answered, thinking it very funny if she were actually my boss, Christ, what would become of me!

We started to walk, past the porter, to catch the very shiny lift up to the 24th floor. We seemed to have completely forgotten about my case as that was still in the boot of the car. Well, I probably didn't need anything tonight anyway, but Kimmi's organizational skills did seem to be in question here. How the hell did she remember to go to work every day, let alone organize other people's schedules? Someone had taken a chance on her that was for sure, I meant, what kind of agency were they?

We reached our floor, ding! The doors opened out onto a long marble corridor, beige and white in complexion dotted with spot lights and the odd pot plant. Pretty to look at but not very well thought out - story of my life really.

We walked on, down the corridor, Kimmi's heels clip clip clopping on the hard marble floor. 'Thank God they haven't polished this thing' she said, taking my arm and pointing towards the floor 'as when they do, in these shoes,' she pointed down to her feet 'I'll go arse over tit' she added. 'No shit!' I replied, thinking this place must be lethal when drunk - what with the floor and these endless corridors that all looked the same - you'd never get out alive!

We finally arrived at the apartment, number 4 on floor 24. Easy to remember and all that. Kimmi started searching in her little Gucci purse for the keys and, amazingly, they were the first thing she came across. We opened the door and let ourselves into the apartment without too much fuss or hassle.

The very smooth and shiny parquet floor opened up to reveal a spacious living area and had obviously just been polished as

Kimmi immediately removed her shoes. I thought it only polite to do the same and followed suit, the both of us now padding around on our tiptoes like a couple of buggerlugs.

Fuck! She pressed a button located to the left of the door like something out of a James Bond film and the electronic shutters started to open to reveal panoramic views of what must have been a four mile long stretch west of Central Park, the only way to see NY I mean, seriously, this shit was breathtaking!

'Here we are', she announced, '105 Riverside Drive baby!' leading me up to the window looking over the park. 'Best kept secret in Manhattan, forget Park Avenue princess. This shit is real, this is where the magic happens, right?' she asked, making her way to an oversized drinks cabinet and pouring us the biggest glasses of what looked to be a good merlot.

'Cheers' she said, handing me a glass.

'A toast is in order I'm sure' I added, clearing my throat. She made her way over to the window to join me. Clinking glasses, we made the traditional eye contact of a toast, 'To love, life and prosperity!' I went on, looking around ironically.

'Oh yes', agreed Kimmi, with a snigger, 'to prosperity oh yeah, I'll certainly drink to that!'

I couldn't tell you how long we were up for, or what time I passed out in the guest bedroom, but sunshine was streaming through the open window when I awoke with a jolt. I could hear voices, some low tones of a deeply masculine voice with a distinctive Brooklyn twang *that must be Marti; he must be getting ready for work.* They sounded very pally with their chit chat. I could hear Kimmi too, she was making him some fresh orange juice from the juicing machine in the kitchen while they chatted.

'Is she awake yet?' I then heard Marti ask Kimmi in a low voice, 'I wanted to see her before I leave after everything you've told me' he added.

'Look, don't wake her babe', Kimmi asked, 'She had a long flight and some wine last night, let her sleep it off, but if you pop your head round her door I'm sure you'll have a good enough view as we forgot to bring her things up from the car last night and she went to bed in my Mickey Mouse t-shirt and not much else!'

I heard him padding down the hallway, looking for his briefcase or something... He then stopped, giving Kimmi a kiss on the mouth, 'Bye sweetie!' and made for the door passing my room on his exit. I heard the footsteps stop - he was obviously thinking about it - taking a look that is.

I heard Kimmi encourage him: 'Go on honey, take a look, she ain't gonna bite ya, she's sleeping baby.'

He took her advice, 'Ok just quickly' and with that I froze, not having time to change position, sticking half an arse out and half of it in the bed, Mickey mouse t-shirt not covering much and my hair having seen better days as it was strung across the pillow. I didn't move and pretended to be asleep; he came close to the bed… I heard someone lightly bend down… I got a strong whiff of Hermes men's after shave and it immediately reminded me of Money. I felt a hand reach out and touch my hair. His hand was soft and warm, and comforting in a strange way as, let's face it, he was a complete stranger to me.

'She's sweet Kimmi', he said in a whisper, 'not sexy like you doll but the girl's got something.'

'Marti, you'll be late for work' I heard Kimmi say in a hushed whisper, 'Let's all catch up later on, she'll be here when you get home' she added, unconvincingly, and with that they were both gone and out the door. Kimmi to the agency and him to the street… Wall Street that is.

Thank God for that! A moment on my own, I let out the air I'd been tightly holding in my lungs and my whole body relaxed in the white feather down duvet. Why, oh why did this shit happen? I'd just got myself into another potentially complicated situation; it was just waiting to happen. Myself, Kimmi and Marti? No, that was not the future.

I needed to get out of this arrangement, as quickly as humanly possible. But first coffee. I couldn't really go anywhere, all of my things were still in the boot of Kimmi's car, the car she drove to work – great planning - and I didn't really know where the fuck I was anyway, apart from where Central Park was, and that's only coz I could see it there, blatantly out the window, hardly a stroke of genius.

I headed for the kitchen; there was a coffee percolator right next to the juicing machine I heard Kimmi use earlier. It looked pretty straight forward too: water in one side, coffee in the other. *Why couldn't everything be this simple?* I mused, switching the thing on and filling it up. I then went to the fridge to get the milk and spotted Kimmi's note:

> *Dear sleeping beauty, as you know, I now have a sort of day job at the agency, or your agency should I say so, anyway, what I propose we do is this: I'll arrange for Marti to send a car for you around midday. It'll pick you up from there and drop you here, the agency, that way you can meet everyone. The agency apartment is not far from here either so we'll go straight from here to there. Borrow some clothes of mine if you need to, the ones you were wearing on the plane have red wine over them from last night. Bottoms may be ok but top, no go - sorry about that! Oh and p.s. Marti says he thinks you're cool. Love ya sweat pea. Auntie Kimmi. X.*

Jesus! This chick didn't mess around! There was no way I was gonna hang out with Marti, flight or no flight, he would just have to put it down to a bad investment.

The other bad news was that if I rocked up to the agency in Kimmi's clothes, they may mistake me for a two bit hooker rather than a fashion model. No, there was only one thing for it: I would have to wear his clothes.

And with that I finished making my coffee, took my peanut butter and banana sandwich and made my way into the bedroom they shared together. Now, where does this fucker keep his clothes… I started to look through: pink shirt no, blue shirt no, yellow shirt no, I was getting nowhere fast but then I spied it, ah yes, here we go… the classic white shirt, yes! Teamed with the black leggings from the plane, and Mickey Mouse underneath the shirt, no one will know.

I sauntered into their en-suite bathroom which, yes you've guessed it, is mostly marble with a mirrored wall all the way around one side. I went to the sink, used a toothbrush (hopefully a spare) and put the shower on, good temperature, great pressure. I got in and started to test the acoustics: 'Biggy, biggy, biggy, can't you see, sometimes your words just hypnotize me!'

Heading to the agency.

The drive from their apartment to the agency seemed long and somewhat tedious with all the traffic, but that was probably more to do with my angst rather than the length of the journey. However, I used this time to recap in my mind what and how much information I knew about this agency.

Well, let's see they were small, independent and had a tendency to hire girls with untapped potential that other agencies passed over – largely due to the fact that they didn't want them or couldn't deal with them. I won't go into it now but you know behavioral problems and others such as... it happened sometimes... anyway, for argument's sake we'll refer to the agency as Gigi's.

Gigi's were a smart agency as they didn't concentrate on fashion. 'There ain't no money in fashion baby' as Kimmi would tell you, no, they made the bulk of their change from advertising as that's what you have to do if you're a small agency and want to stay afloat.

The other trump card they had, an ex-supermodel with a troubled past. I'm not sure if she had been fired from her former agency or just got sick of the autocracy that comes with working for any large organization, either way, she had left them to come here. Smart move if you ask me, as these peeps had perks I mean, just look at the picture of their apartment I had in my pocket!

We were now cruising down Park Avenue South. I pulled out the crumpled piece of paper Kimmi had left me on the fridge as it had the address of the agency on the other side. Yeah ok, we were very close, 109 Park Av. South it said.

The driver pulled up to the left of the side walk, 'We're here' he announced, '5th floor, do you want me to wait?' he asked.

'Mmhmm, no' I replied, 'It's best that you go as I've no idea how long I'm gonna be or if Kimmi's taking me to the apartment after here'.

'No problem' he said and with that I got out and he drove off.

I took a glimpse of myself in the mirror of the lift as it made its way up to the 5th floor. *Fuck, should have brushed my hair!* Apart from that, not bad considering the lack of effort and all that. As the lift doors opened, I walked out to find myself in a plush but boring looking New York agency. They didn't seem overwhelmingly busy which I quite liked as some of these places resemble mayhem when entering.

Kimmi greeted me first, jumping up from her chair and throwing her arms in the air in an overly elaborate fashion. 'Supermodel!' she trilled obviously for effect as it was more than obvious to anyone that knew me that my lack of dedication in the industry - not to mention lack of talent - would never lead to such a ridiculous status however, I let her have her moment.

Boss man Douglas then got up from his chair, at least I presumed it was him, and sauntered over to me. ' Hey there, English' he said, extending a hand to meet mine. He looked like a geek at best and a weirdo at worst, with very black facial hair just around his mouth, round glasses and a short black curly haircut, what could only be described asymmetrical.

He managed to overcome these less than appealing looks by his cool, city slicker aura which seemed to encapsulate him in a bubble. I had to double take for a minute or so… was this guy for real? It was like watching something out of a bad Woody Allen film.

'So, English,' he went on in a very strong east coast accent, 'what do ya weigh?'

'What do you mean what do I weigh?' I replied. 'What kind of question is that?'

'It's a question I ask models.' he went on, 'It's irrelevant how much I weigh, what I weigh doesn't change things, I still get paid regardless of how fat my arse is, but you English, you need to be the right weight before we can do anything with you'. He went out of the room and came back with a pair of weighing scales, 'So this is what we do, we weigh you. Come on English, hop on!' He placed them down on the floor not far from my feet.

'You've got to be kidding me.' I went on 'What is this shit?' I looked from him to Kimmi then back to him again; it was no use. They were both adamant that I should get on the scales.

The result was not good.

'What in Jesus's name have you been eating English? This is ridiculous! This is off the radar!'

Kimmi bent down to see exactly what the scales said. 'Wowser!' she remarked 'This ain't good babe.' She stepped back again.

Unfortunately it was Douglas's turn to talk again. He cleared his throat 'This is well over your proposed weight English. I mean wowser! Sorry to quote Kimmi but it's amazing and not in a good way! I mean, you don't even look this heavy but, but there's no denying it, you are and...' he paused again 'I mean Jesus Christ English, you make the Queen Mother look like an athlete!'

I moved around to the other side of the room and took a seat, hoping it would deter me from physical violence towards him. My mind started reeling: I'd never had any weight problems in the past; I'd always been classed as slim but... I stood up and looked at myself in the full length mirror, front ways, then sideways. I sat down again deflated. You know what? They had a point.

I had the beginnings of a tiny pot belly. Money said it was cute and it never really bothered me.

The face... ok, that was a little puffy... too much alcohol and late nights... but I could fix that, right?

The arse, ok a little large... but that was my build, right? I couldn't help that!

I was trying to convince myself now as much as anyone else... but it was no use... I'd let myself slip... there were no two ways about it... my eyes started to swell with tears... *What do I do now? Go home?*

I turned to Douglas. He turned to Kimmi. 'What do we do with her peeps?' he asked, clutching Kimmi's arm in mock desperation.

'Oh stop it Doggie!' she replied, 'This is no time for jokes'. Kimmi came over and gave me a squeeze.

'Now,' she began, 'We can fix this. No crying over a fat arse.'

'Ok, ok' I replied, feeling like an idiot.

'This is what we do' she started to rummage through her little black address book, got a number, picked up the phone at the desk and started to dial. 'Yes, hello' she said in her best phone voice to whoever it was on the other end of the receiver 'is that Bunny Fitness? Oh good I'd like to register a new member.'

She got me the special model membership which the agency get at discounted rate as it's only available off peak on week days, which still left the whole weekend to get through without drinking and partying. I was not sure that was possible...

'Now' began Douglas, two steps ahead of me as ever, 'I'm quite happy for you Kimmi to take English on as your little project and for her to stay if she's willing to put the work in but it's Friday today and I'm not having you two girls tearing up NY for the next few days getting rat-arsed at my expense! It ain't happening peeps' he said looking at both of us. 'I want to see planned structured activity: something outside, something active. No nightclubs ok?'

'Oh come on doogie-woogie' Kimmi went on, in her best baby doll voice, 'It's her first weekend in NY! We wanna...'

He interrupted, 'and you wanna nothing. No, no, no.' He stopped her dead. 'You know the rules sweet cheeks, it's my way or the highway' and with that he left the office.

I looked to Kimmi and Kimmi back to me. I spoke first 'We can do this, right Kimmi Star?' really looking for her support right now. There's a long silence as she moves her way around to the other side of the desk, towards the office fridge. I looked at my watch, almost 4pm. She reached inside the fridge and poured herself a large Jack Daniels and coke, and started swirling it around with her finger.

'Yeah babe,' she said sipping on her drink, completely unaware that this was the last thing she should be doing in a helpful sense right now, 'It'll be no problem.'

Central Park Upper West Side.

People always talk about the ethereal quality of light in places like Africa and the Far East but I was sure they had never seen NY at dawn, as nothing really prepared you for that, or could be compared to it should I say.

It was as if the world of infrastructure, streets, buildings and bodies came strangely to a halt - silence - with all the city people out of sight. We were bathed (Kimmi and I) in a dim emerald blanket of light. It was hard to describe but it made the city feel as if the place were not reality anymore, but more of an aura, a presence. It had that piece of magic, like falling in love I s'pose.

I looked down at the glow from my cigarette and then put it out. Enough about things I knew nothing about, I told myself. On to the serious task at hand: finding the stables, Claremont Riding Academy to be precise, on the Upper West Side.

We were walking through the park now, Central Park, not far from the bridle path. 'This place must be here somewhere' piped up Kimmi after a long silence, the two of us still feeling shell shocked after a very early supper with Douglas last night. At his request, we both stayed at the agency apartment leaving Marti seething over his dry Martini back at their apartment. Tough love and all that, as Kimmi would say. Anyway, Douglas had kindly (or unkindly depending on how you look at it) set the alarm clock for 6 in the morning to get us down to the stables in time for the first ride of the day. So here we were.

'What are your riding abilities?' asked the man in charge of the stables, 'Can you both ride?' he asked, looking us up and down.

'Well,' I began first, 'I used to ride a lot a few years back' I said, patting the horse he had just allocated me, 'so I'm sure it'll all come back to me'.

'Very good' he said, handing me the saddle and expecting me to put it on. 'And you?' he asked, pointing at Kimmi, 'What are your riding skills like?'

'Oh' said Kimmi, looking at me, more animated now 'there ain't nothing I can't ride' she said with a cheeky smile.

'Oh man', I sighed out loud, 'this is gonna be a long morning'.

She took her saddle from the man and leading her horse outside we both mounted up. This is when I began to get slightly nervous as Kimmi had persuaded the stables that we were both such expert riders that we would not be needing any assistance during our ride, and to let us go off independently without any guidance, back up or insurance come to think of it... How do these things happen?

We started off at a leisurely trot, I let Kimmi take the lead and I followed in behind her, just to make sure she could actually ride. So far so good.

The 843 acre rectangle open space of park had now opened up in front of us... Wow! It really was immense, an oasis from the insanity. We passed lush lawns, flowering gardens and glassy puddles of water on the now meandering, wooded path we had taken. Kimmi's horse, which was a good foot taller than mine (at her request) - in fact it could easily have been a stallion, strong and skittish it seemed – would probably flinch at any little breaking of a twig under foot, or yelp of a dog barking. Not a great sign all in all but she seemed unconcerned, which actually was of little comfort at this point.

It was easy to get carried away with the majestic beauty of it all, looking around us, but I was forced to remind myself that everything, from the lawns to the lakes to the forest at the north, was man-made.

Talking about forest, we must have reached the north of the park as it was coming up to our left.

'Kim... Kimmi!' I attempted to shout out as the path began to veer off, in the direction of the forest. 'Don't take that path, it's too off the beaten track, stick to the right and head off towards the lakes!'

'KIMMI!' I shouted now as her horse appeared to be getting faster and faster, what the fuck! Her horse suddenly broke into a canter! She didn't look in control, but it was too soon to say whether she was in trouble or not. However, for me to catch her now, I would have had to break into a full on gallop and that was not going to happen.

Jesus! Her horse had broken into a full on gallop, now rearing up its front hooves in the air and heading straight into the forest like a wild thing… nooooo!

There was nothing I could do… I slowed down and came to a standstill, hoping she would regain control of her horse and come back to find me. Chance would be a fine thing. I dismounted and looked at the time: wow, we'd already been out a good 45 minutes, where did the time go?

We'd have to return to the stables in 15 minutes anyway. *God my arse aches, oh Douglas will be pleased*, at least that's a good thing as pain meant exercise and I'd definitely got some of that!

I turned around to attempt to lead the horse back to the stables, wherever that may be, when I noticed there was a man watching me. I turned my back to him, giving him time to realize that staring at me, with this horse, on this day of all days, was a bad idea and he should probably get lost.

He was still standing there. Ok, that was it. I let ripe on him, just in the mood for some verbal annihilation: 'Look you fat fuck, it's time to get lost, ok, the shows over, fuck off!'

'Tobacco' he said, completely unperturbed, presenting me a hand to shake, 'Jamas Tobacco. Lovely to meet you' he added with a silly smile. I unwillingly shook his hand. 'And you must be?' he added.

'Oh yeah, right', I replied, still completely uncommitted to any polite form of conversation, 'I'm a charming English girl, who wants to know?'

'Well' said Jamas, still as smug and smarmy as ever, 'I'm a film director you know, you may have heard of me?'

'No' I answered quickly 'Can't say I have'.

'Well, anyway' he went on, 'have you ever done any acting?' he went on, 'I mean', he started laying it on thick now, 'you're so magnetic, I couldn't stop watching you there for a second.'

'Well try to stop yourself' I shot back, still unconvinced of his credentials.

He went on 'You have such a strong presence; I know a star when

I see one he added.'

'Oh I've heard that before,' I said, 'right before someone tries to have sex with me. Look, thank you but no thanks. I've got things to do like find my booker who's flown off on a horse somewhere… and loose this fat arse before I lose my contract, so sorry but I need to be off.'

'Wait! Wait! He said, 'so you're a model right?' 'Kind of,' I went on, 'I'm on a sort of model probation at the moment.'

'Oh don't worry about that,' he said, 'being a model is a mugs game anyway' he added.

Yeah tell me about it, I couldn't have agreed more at this point. 'I agree.' I finally said giving him eye contact for the first time in our conversation.

'Look, here's my number.' He wrote it down on a piece of paper. 'I want to screen test you next week for a film I have in mind. Wardy Beats in it too, you heard of Wardy Beats, right?'

'Right' I said, still thinking this guy's full of shit.

'Ok, make sure you call me.'

I took the piece of paper, took a look at the local number and put it in my pocket. 'I'll give it to my agency,' I replied, 'and they will call you, ok?' I added.

'No, no, no,' he said with a sigh, 'I'm up to my neck will damn model agencies, it's a no go, and they're a pain in the arse! You call me directly and we arrange the screen test or no go. That's the way it goes in the industry. Ok kid?'

I paused, not thinking about what he was saying to me at all now, but thinking about Money. *Money would call me Kid all the time; it was his word, his pet name for me, not this jerk's! Who the fuck was he? How dare he use that line? It sounded so wrong when he said it.* I decided right then and there that he was an arse hole and should be treated accordingly.

'Look, I may call you, I may not,' leading my horse away from him, 'That's the way it goes in my industry.' I replied, mocking him now 'Ciao!' and with that I was off.

Back at the apartment, 8 p.m.

It was late when I got back to the agency apartment, 62nd and Broadway, just off Columbus which, compared to Kimmi and Marti's place, looked somewhat average. With no phone to inform anyone of what happened, I arrived to find Douglas pacing up and down the kitchen/living area.

'What the hell happened English?' he said with disbelief, as I skulked through the door really not in the mood for his authoritarian presence.

'I lost Kimmi.' I replied, 'Her horse went mad, galloped off into the forest, leaving me with some pervert film director trying to look at my arse. So no, not the most successful horse riding expedition in the world but anyway, how are you? How was your day?'

He looked at me with a totally new found exasperation and completely discounting my question to him. He sat me down at the round table facing the window that is usually reserved for serious chats and such like, and went to the kitchen where something had obviously been cooking. 'We're having chicken and broccoli' he informed me in a low tone, bringing it to the table, a plate for him and one for myself.

He then poured us both a small glass of white wine to accompany the meal, breaking his own rules I noted, but I'd have been foolish to bring that up. I spread one of the napkins that had been left on the table for me across my lap and we both began to eat, silently. The chicken was very good, tender.

Douglas spoke first: 'I found Kimmi,' he said, 'she managed to regain control of her horse and get it out the forest but by that time couldn't find you and made her way back to the stables. She then had to dash off back to Marti's as it's her night to work at The Hustler and she needed to get ready.'

'Oh yeah,' I replied, 'I forgot it was her club night'.

'But anyway,' he added, 'she's fine and will be back in the office Monday morning.' He then tucked into his chicken as if he'd been waiting to get this information out the way before he could digest his food.

I took a sip of my wine, Jewish tasting I thought, not that I knew much about wine but Douglas was Jewish, so I presumed it must be, or perhaps it was just because there wasn't very much of it.

Anyway, I got back to the conversation: 'About this…'

He interrupted, obviously reading my trail of thought, 'What was his name?' he asked seriously, 'The film producer.'

'Jamas,' I replied, 'Jamas Tobacco'.

Douglas took a long sip of his wine.

'Oh no,' he went on, 'not this guy.' He leaned back on his chair looking thoughtful but careworn.

'This guy is the biggest pervert in the film industry' he said, stretching his legs out and flinging his glasses down on the table, 'not to mention a pimp for Wardy Beat.' he added, now stretching his arms above his head looking anode but still slightly interested. 'I can't believe he's still in operation, after all these years' he added, rubbing his tired eyes.

'What does he want you to do?' he added, now resting his head between his hands, elbows on the table.

'Well,' I began, 'he wants me to go down town to an audition studio first thing Monday morning and try out for a new film that Wardy Beat, he says, is going to be in.'

'Oh bullshit' said Douglas butting in, 'this guy makes Kimmi's friend Marti look like a Christian, I mean seriously English, you're not even thinking about going, right?'

'I've not given it any thought yet.' I said, lying through my teeth, 'Anyway, what do you think about it all?' I asked him, not expecting such an explicit answer…

Well he went on: 'If you were to go, which you most certainly are not, English, I'd expect you'd be asked to go and stand behind some sort of screen. It would be dark so you would not be able to see exactly who would be in the room with you.'

'Who would be in the room?' I asked, curious.

'Well' he answered, topping up his own wine and not mine - he then caught a glimpse of my unimpressed expression – 'It's for your own good English, trust me' and then, back to the story: 'Where was I, ah yes, I should imagine in the room with you would be Wardy Beat, on the other side of the screen, naturally. You wouldn't be able to see him as that's what the screen is designed for.'

'What would he be doing?' I asked, 'and how do you know all this?' I added, looking at him suspiciously.

'Look English', he went on, 'It doesn't matter how I know all this but it's lucky for you that I do. So anyway, Mr. Beat would then instruct Tobacco to instruct you to take your clothes off, all the while Beat gets off on it in any way he can. Please don't ask me to elaborate.' he added, but there was no chance of me asking him to do that, I had already heard more than enough.

I took my last sip of wine, draining the glass. With so much information to take in and such a long day as I had had, the tiredness hit me like a pane of glass.

'Do you mind if I go to bed?' I asked him, giving his hand a squeeze as he went to light up a cigarette, 'It's been a long day.'

'Yeah, no problem English, I'll clean up here' he added, gesturing towards the plates.

I thanked him for dinner as I got up to leave the table, he got up too, lighting his cigarette and taking it out into the living area which was all dark wood, art books and fresh flowers. I headed off to the main model bedroom which luxuriously I had all to myself, well for tonight anyway. I lightly shut the door behind me.

Saturday morning 9.45 am. New York City.

I awoke with a jolt, as per usual, but something was different this morning: I just couldn't move. I attempted to get up and move around, but it was no use.

It hurt when I sat down; it hurt when I stood up. Wow, at this rate, I would need to shower in my pajamas, as removing them would involve more pain than I was in already. I kept telling myself there was some sort of perverse pleasure in this pain and I was really enjoying it however, this was such a far-fetched lie I couldn't even tell it to myself. I decided right there and then that I were never going horse riding again. Fact.

I made my way into the kitchen area to make breakfast. There was a picture of a random very fat person stuck to the front of the fridge, thank you Douglas, as if I needed reminding that in fashion terms, I was as fat as a house.

I removed the fat free milk from the fridge and then looked for a suitable complement: Weetabix no, Coco Pops no, Kellogg's Special K, too obvious a choice, and then I spotted them, my all-time favorites... Sugar Puffs, oh yeah! I poured not too large a portion into a bowl, added the totally tasteless milk and went to sit my aching arse down at the round window table we were sat last night. It was not until that moment that I realized that the phone in the living area was ringing off the hook and that I should go and answer it.

'Hullo' I said, mouthful of Sugar Puffs, 'that you Douglas?' Considering it couldn't be anyone else calling for me, seeing as it was obvious he wasn't in the apartment.

'Yeah English, it's me. Listen, I'm not far from Time Square on my way to a meeting, a meeting with a very talented photographer; she's well known and respected in the industry. Now, I wouldn't normally be having a meeting like this on a Saturday but English, she is very interested in working with a new girl in town'.

'Oh yes?' I said, intrigued.

'An English one, carrying a few extra pounds, unbelievably' he added.

'Oh shut up Douglas I responded, I'm not that overweight!'

'Anyway' he went on, 'It's for tomorrow, if I can sort it, you in?'

'What does she want me to do?' I asked.

'Well,' he went on, 'She just wants to test you for now but I'm sure it will lead to something more later on.'

I thought for a moment...

Testing is when a good photographer takes test shots of you purely for the purpose of 'building your book' which means adding something credible to your portfolio to show you and the photographers creative potential for future clients.

'You can do it English' he added, 'just say yes.'

Well, I started to think to myself, my book could really do with improving and in the past I had worked well with female photographers. 'Yes' I replied 'and thanks Douglas'.

'No problem English' and with that he was gone.

Early morning Sunday, Upper West Side.

She didn't introduce herself when opening the studio door, she didn't need to, I knew exactly who she was and her me.

She led me up a set of very steep steps, which led up to her fifth floor apartment and a large and expansive roof terrace that shot out from behind the building. She must have owned this also as I didn't see how anyone else could have access to it, the only way out there was through the back of the kitchen. The apartment was beautiful, there was no denying it.

This woman obviously had a lot of money, and some very expensive tastes: I spied a Van Gogh hanging in the hallway, and another picture from the well-known artist Frida Kahlo just resting on the mantel, the picture is of a lady giving birth by the looks of things. I looked more closely, oh, ok, the lady giving birth also has no head, mmhmm, interesting…

Behind me were the double French doors that led out onto the roof… to check out later I thought to myself, and lit up a ciggie, Marlboro, naturally. That's when she came to join me brandishing an ashtray.

'That's where we'll be shooting' she said, making a gesture towards the terrace. 'The light's amazing later on' she added. I believed her, I could see from here the view that stretched over the length of Manhattan.

She offered me a drink, of the non-alcoholic variety. I was sure; however, I could bend her to my demand, something I picked up off Kimmi no doubt. I was also more aware than most of what people wanted from me, professionally or personally and, in this case, this cat was in: she wanted to hang out, I could tell.

'I'll have a Jack Daniels and coke please, don't forget the ice!' I added, seeing how far I could push it. She obliged me immediately, sending her assistant come makeup artist into the kitchen to fetch the drinks, hers being the same request as mine: double shot, full fat coke, plenty of ice.

She must have been around her mid-forties or somewhere thereabouts, with cropped chocolate brown hair and a gentle cascading fringe that framed her face perfectly. A face and bone structure so neat, perfect and delicately put together, it could easily have got there through artificial means and probably was, attractive all the same though. Her hands were those of an artist: long, elegant and delicate fingers, and very slim wrists which were a contrast from her strong, long, strapping body. It seemed to command attention, from every angle, whatever she was doing.

She then walked over to the Bang and Olufsen music system and put on a band I knew well, not American either. I was surprised she knew it but really everything about her was surprising.

Her assistant, young, attractive and a little too interested in what I was doing beckoned me over to a makeup chair by the window, opposite a big stage mirror with lights around it. Anywhere else this would have looked tacky but here, in this setting; it looked chic and slightly cool, a bit like her really, the photographer.

The assistant got to work on my face, patting concealer down under my eyes in preparation for the foundation to sit on top. These things take time and I was glad of the Jack Daniels and coke to pass my time.

I looked over to the photographer. She had cranked the music up, drink in hand, and was whirling around, middle of the room. I couldn't take my eyes off her, something that would make any other person look like a fool made her look cool; she was stylish man, that's for sure. She got out silver vile of coke from her jeans pocket and put it up to her nose taking a sniff. Wow, Douglas would not approve, I thought to myself, a smile seeping across my face.

She had found me a Givenchy dress to wear, one of hers I'm sure as we were roughly around the same size.

'What do you think?' she said holding it out to me.

'Let's see' I said as I never really knew if anything was going to fit me until I tried it on.

I slipped my clothes off and handed them to the makeup artist/assistant, who liked me even less by this point and looked on disapprovingly.

'Wait', said the photographer, 'let's get you on the roof terrace first'. I led the way with the photographer behind me, clutching the dress and a pair of Malono Blahnik. Douglas must have told her my size, I thought to myself, behind her came Miss Make up/assistant holding a big Lexus camera and light reflector. This was the norm.

I am now stood outside in a tiny G-string and some Manolo Blahnik heals with a view of the Manhattan sky line behind me. The light was breathtaking.

I reached out my arm and took the dress from her; she was staring at my breasts… The dress fitted perfectly. I went and stood to the far end of the wall, buildings behind me. She had not told me to but after enough shoots in the business, you get a feel for what will work. I turned side on and we started to shoot. She worked quickly and so did I as the light was fading now and this was the moment to get it. We finished just as quickly as we had started.

She told me I was good.

'That's what they all say' I responded, walking up to her and, taking the coke out her pocket, I took a sniff, 'mmhmm not bad' I said and handed it back.

She looked shocked but amused.

We walked inside, make up assistant behind me, but then I felt an arm reach out and grab my hand. It was the makeup artist, she wanted a word with me in the kitchen: 'I s'pose you think you're funny' she went on. 'I don't know what you mean' I answered, 'I don't think I'm anything babe' I said, removing her grip from my arm and drinking my Jack Daniels casually.

I pushed past her, *God what was up with this chick?* I thought, going back inside the living area. I went and sat down on the sofa; the photographer came and sat next to me while the makeup artist cleared up makeup shit.

'I don't think she likes me very much' I said to the photographer, pouring myself another drink, who replied with a naughty grin as she knew exactly who I was talking about.

'Oh well', she finally answered, 'that figures', she added playing with my hair.

'How is that?' I said, now feeling a little uncomfortable and moving away from her.

'She's my girlfriend.' she added, reaching in towards me and stroking my breast...

The makeup artist was looking on watching us as if she knew that this was on the cards.

Oh fuck! I thought to myself, *this is not what I'm into...*

I thought fast. 'Can I borrow your phone?' I said with a smile but gently removing her hand.

'Yeah darling' she replied, 'it's just down the hallway'.

Thank fuck for that! I was thinking, and quickly got up, getting Kimmi's mobile number out of my pocket and hurrying to the hallway.

...07.... I dialed the number, she picked up, thank God.

'Kim, Kimmi', I said breathlessly,

'Hey doll' she responded, 'What's up?'

'Where are you?' I said urgently... 'I'm coming to meet...'

'No problem sweets' she said, giving the address of an office block in Time Square. Strange, I thought to myself, what was she doing there?

But no time for questions now, she could hear the urgency in my voice and added 'Just jump in a cab babe and I'll pay, you're on Park Avenue right?'

'Right' I responded, Douglas must have told her I was testing here. 'I'm coming right now I added, I'll bring wine' and with that, I was gone.

5th avenue, 4th, I was counting them down now, the cab driver was travelling at speed however, he couldn't get me there fast enough. I cracked open the wine I'd picked up from the off license some way up the block. I was lucky they didn't I.D. me as you have to be 21 here to drink. I know, outrageous, but anyway... I was just glad I'd got out of that apartment... that was the main thing. Now to find Kimmi.

Contacting Douglas was out of the question, he'd only blame me for the whole situation and anyway, a little out of order he hadn't actually informed me the photographer was a full on lesbian with a psychotic girlfriend in tow, I meant, Jesus, hardly a relaxing Sunday in New York now was it? And this was before I found out what Kim star was up to!

We were weaving our way through Time Square now, which brought a whole new meaning to the word traffic, I tell you. He was beeping and shouting like crazy, which is pretty insignificant really as all the other cab drivers in a 10 mile radius were beeping and shouting also. The cab driver turned round to throw a few words in my direction 'Worst time of day this is Missy, always like this, always the same', he added lighting up a ciggie and smoking it out the driver's side window.

That's what I needed to do; smoke away this angst the whole experience had left in my stomach. I wound down the window of the passenger's side and stuck my head out.

I could see the block I was heading for as the numbers were clearly written on the side of the buildings. I gathered my belongings which mainly consisted of wine, added a touch of lippy to go with my already full on makeup from the shoot, paid the cabbie and told him I'd walk the remaining block on foot as this traffic was now at a standstill. 'Ok Missy' he responded, giving me a quick glance in his rear view mirror and with that I got out the cab.

We were smack bang in the middle of Midtown Manhattan, this area around the intersection of Broadway and 7th Avenue had become so intertwined with NYC in the minds of non-New Yorkers that regardless of how dignified it had become, it was still considered quintessential New York.

However for me, right now, it was just a crossroads. I stopped, lit up a Marlboro from my pocket. This relaxed me slightly, as long as I didn't look up and grasped how utterly small and insignificant I was next to these tall and looming buildings which seemed to be closing in on me like some out of control virus.

I walked a little, passing dozens of Broadway theatres located between 41st and 54th Street between 6th and 9th Avenues. Every single one was trying to compete with its money-making rivals next door, the capitalist site of the world, oh *how Groucho Marx would be impressed!* I couldn't help but wonder as I outed my ciggie.

I finally located the office block I was looking for and stepped off the sidewalk, entering through some double glass doors. The intercom was right in front of me and I pressed the appropriate buzzer… buzz… buzz…

'Hey doll!' I heard Kimmi's voice booming out of the intercom. She obviously had got camera ID on the other side otherwise there was no way she would have known it was me. I heard the electric noise of the door unlock from the other side so I pushed the door to the left of me and it opened inwards. 'Come on up!' I heard her call, 'I'm in the middle of a call', and with that I strolled through the lobby of the building. There was no porter in sight so I made my way straight to the elevator which was hardly hard to find as it was right there in front of me.

I got in, pushed the button for the 4th floor and let the lift take me up. Pretty fancy setup I thought to myself as I was transported to the 4th floor in a haze of black shiny tiles and delicately positioned lighting, the kind designed to make everyone look a good 10 years younger than their actual age, not that I needed that just yet, but good to know all the same...

However, right now, I was more intrigued to know exactly what Kimmi was doing here as you can bet your life on the fact that Douglas knew nothing of this little set up, that was for sure. No, this looked like a distinctly Kimmi style operation if ever I'd seen one... what the hell was she up to now?

Ding! I stepped out of the lift and onto what looked to be some sort of well-polished wooden floor, very chic, yet like most incredibly shiny things, incredibly slippy. What was it with Kimmi and slippy floors? I asked myself, thinking of her and Marti's apartment block (same problem with that too).

I'd followed the directions she'd given me once inside but this couldn't be right? This was leading me into some kind of office suite; what would she be doing here at this time of night? For it was coming up to 9pm now and even I knew that ain't office hours, even in this town.

I tentatively pushed open the door to reveal a large, carpeted office room containing a leather couch to the right side of the room, running almost the length of it as you entered, and a long rosewood table to the middle consisting of telephone, many of them, a fax machine, ash trays, some used, some not, a dell laptop and several bottles of JD and coke miniature - Kimmi's favorite. She'd obviously been here a while as they were all empty, all five of them.

Kimmi was sat with her back to me behind the desk, cigarette in hand, chatting all kinds of ridiculous nonsense to some poor fool on the other end of the receiver. This was just too much information for a Sunday evening… I mean… what the fuck was going on here?

The phones were ringing off the hook, first one, then the other, then her mobile, all going off in unison. She answered the one on the desk first 'Hello, Manhattan Limits' she purrs down the receiver, 'can I help you? Oh hey toots! I was just thinking about you!' she giggled. Tonight? Yeah sure, no problem, I have the perfect one for you. Yeah, she's…'

I switched off by this point, it was obvious what Kimmi's new little side line was and I wanted no part of it; so if she thought she was roping me in she could forget it. Moving over to the window where the glasses are kept on a little shelf, I removed two wine glasses and took them over to the desk where Kimmi was still making her pitch to whoever it was on the phone.

I got the white wine from my bag and poured us a large glass each, leaving hers on the desk and taking mine over to where the sofa was and sat down. Well, there was only one way to get through this evening and that was to drink through it without a doubt. I slipped my shoes off and hook my toes over one end of the sofa, reclining my body back to stretch over the length of it and my head propped up the other end. My dress all ruffled up around my ass looking far more hucci than Gucci at this point however I was past caring.

I took a large sip of wine and listened to the bullshit in motion. She was pretty good at it, I had to admit.

"Manhattan Limits' she took another call. Wow, she must have booked quite a few jobs in the short space of time I'd been here. *God, there's some real suckers out there*, getting drunker by the minute on my very empty stomach.

Glancing over in my direction she quickly put a hand over the receiver and leaned in to make a comment under her breath 'Someone's getting lit!', she looked the length of me with a laugh (lit is NY slang for getting wasted).

'I have to do this Kimmi' I responded, 'to put up with your bullshit!' I added with a smile and with that she drained her glass too.

'Well you can't have all the fun can you?' she added, 'you wait till I've finished my shift. Paaaarrrrty, oh yeah!' She went to put some music on and then suddenly remembered something important: 'Oh crap' she went on, 'oh hell no, what time is it?' she asked.

I looked at my watch '10.45 pm babe, why?'

'Oh crap!' she exclaimed, 'There's a girl coming to try out for the agency. I need to interview her, you know, see if she's right.'

'Ok' I responded, 'what time is she coming?'

She shot me a worried look 'Right about now' she added.

'Oh brilliant, I'm fucking lit and you're not much better yourself!' I said looking into her dilated pupils.

'We'll get through it' she said unconvincingly, 'just try to act straight, ok, no wise cracks English' she added in a silly Douglas accent.

'Yeah, right!' I laughed, 'and no bullshit from you Miss Kimstar' I went on.

However, she didn't have time to respond as just at that moment the intercom went.

'Oh!' I said excitedly, 'let the fun and games begin!'

And with that, Kimmi pressed the button on the intercom to let her in. I, on the other hand, added another coat of Chanel lippy, attempted to stand up without falling over and straightened out my dress, which at this stage had seen better days. *Yes, that should do it*, I thought to myself,

'Looking good girl!' Kimmi added with a snigger and with that she walked in…

I should have known, I should have guessed the moment I saw her that something was amiss; the chick just wasn't who she said she was but call it blind stupidity or blame it on the booze, I just didn't for the life of me foresee what was unfolding right before my eyes, the defining moment just before everything imploded. The beginning of the end as it were.

'Would you like a drink?' Kimmi offered her in a way too enthusiastic tone, fetching the last and only clean glass remaining on the window sill and filling it from the bottle of wine we were drinking from.

'No thank you' said the Puerto Rican looking girl, refusing the glass and glancing down at the pager she had clutched in her hand. 'I'm driving' she said, looking at me nervously as I plonked myself down on the sofa taking the wine from Kimmi that Miss Puerto Rican had refused, and starting to drink it.

'Helps me think you see' I told her, or so I'd been telling myself all these years. There was no response from Puerto Rican chick.

With my other free hand I slapped the seat on the sofa beside me in a gesture for her to sit down, and took this opportunity to take a better look at this chick, up close, which wasn't all that, let me tell you…

She did as I had asked and plonked her 5'3 arse down next to mine with some trepidation, naturally, as anyone who wasn't anyone's fool could have told you we were two loose cannons in this room right now, and without so much as a hint of provocation, either of us could go off at any time.

'Come on sister' I said slapping her arse inappropriately, 'show us what ya got'.

Kimmi started to snigger as Puerto Rican girl looked to the floor mortified, which I found slightly confusing as, let's face it, the girl had supposedly rocked up to be the new pretty woman in town, hardly a status driven position.

But anyway, I continued with my relentless campaign of total disrespect: 'Show me your arse' I said, with a big smile, reaching out to touch her. She started to back away from me, moving further and further up the other end of the sofa. 'I… I…' her words were stumbling now. In fact, she was lost for them.

Kimmi then took this opportunity to take over the leadership role in our mindless operation: 'Look girlfriend', she went on, 'you gonna show us what you're workin with', a line stolen from one of infamous rap cd's. I put it on, as she had left the particular cd in the music player from earlier.

I walked off to the window, refilled my glass, then cranked it up.

Kimmi got to her feet, standing a few feet away from Miss Puerto Rican, and got prepared to give the poor girl some sort of imitation lap dance, grinding her arse just a few millimeters away from the young woman's nose. De de de... di di.... We're both singing the lyrics now, Kimmi and I, 'shake your ass... what yourself... shake your ass... show us what you're working with...'

Miss Puerto Rican appeared not to be now feeling it at all and, in a surprisingly bold move, got up to leave, or so we thought.

'Hey sister,' spoke up Kimmi, 'you can't be leaving the party yet, we're just getting started and anyway, we've not discussed work yet!' She reached out an arm to her, in an attempt at earnestness, however the two of us were far too gone now for any chance of a sensible discussion, which I think she realised way back before 'shake your ass' came on the stereo.

Just at that moment her pager went off, which seemed to (strangely) send her into more of a panic than our less than perfect behaviour. 'I... I've ... I've got to move my car' she finally got the words out, 'I won't be long' she added, 'it's just round the corner' and with that she turned to me, offering only a weak smile by means of explanation and bopped out the door.

'Well', I exclaimed looking at Kimmi, incredulously, 'what a rude bitch!' and with that we both fell about the place, the situation by that time was just too much to handle…

But then the other alarming event of the evening took place: the buzzer went again…

'For fucks sake!' exclaimed Kimmi, 'this bitch is a glutton for punishment!' and with that we absentmindedly buzzed in what we thought to be Miss Puerto Rican through the door. How wrong could Kimmi and I be for Miss Puerto Rican was not at all what she appeared to be…

I can honestly say, I had no inkling at this point, I mean, why should I? I had just rocked up for an innocent drink after almost being molested by a lesbian photographer…

This was Kimmi's gig, not mine, I was just an innocent bystander. In fact, I shouldn't have even been there, what the hell was I doing there in the first place?

However, this was not some bunch of questions I would just have to ask myself, oh no, this bunch of questions I could possibly be asked soon by someone slightly more official than myself, or Kimmi, and that special someone, unfortunately for us, may even be a judge.

Yep, that's right, we were busted, as Miss Puerto Rican was not only our bitch no. 1, oh no, she also turned out to be an undercover police officer. Exactly, double oh no... We were properly fucked now, that was for sure.

As the door flew off its hinges, I saw Kimmi making a dive towards the table which quite obviously had been used to sniff cocaine on during the course of the evening, just to add some extra excitement to our already mounting problems. She got her head as near to the table as possible and gave it an almighty blow...

Thank God for that! As this one move managed to disburse the remnants of white power into the air just in time, as it was at that moment that the bedlam began...

These fuckers were not messing around, that was for sure...

'Don't move!' came the first gun touting male undercover cop's booming voice.

'Get down on the floor!' I then heard a second officer behind him, hot on his heels and just as serious.

He was surveying the room, like dogs staking out their territory.

He reached Kimmi and, fast as lightning, he had her up against the wall. 'Hands above your head Missy'. She was handcuffed and searched as the other cops got to work on the room, removing any small pieces of evidence they could find and putting the offending items in a clear plastic bag.

And now it was my turn, yet I saw a different officer coming for me. *Oh no, you got to be kidding me!* It was Miss Puerto Rican, now baying for my blood after the routine humiliation I pulled on her earlier. Not forgetting any of it, she sauntered over to me. 'Hands against the wall you English idiot' she instructed me as she began her rough and aggressive search of my body. She pulled my arms in front of my body with much more strength and force than was necessary. 'Not too smart now are we Miss Thing?' she said, giving me the once over, 'I'm gonna find a charge for you, that's for sure' she added with an aggressive sort of chuckle, 'You wait and see'.

Funnily enough I believed her as they led us completely unnecessarily out of the building and into a riot van no less, and for those of you that have not had the experience of travelling in one of these vehicles, they sober you up quite quickly, that's for sure.

Not only were we handcuffed, but they also decided to shackle our feet together with a heavy metal chain. Why I didn't know. I thought it best not to ask right now and kept my silence, as did Kimmi who, as I glanced into her face momentarily, looked utterly petrified. All I could detect from her demeanor was the sheer terror of what was to be in store for us. Thank God I had no idea as if I had, I'm sure I'd have been pretty terrified too.

We were headed to the biggest precinct in the whole of

Manhattan, which was a pretty disgusting place to be by anyone's standards and that was in day light hours. However, we were to be arriving in the middle of the night and God only knew what was to come...

The cop that led me out the van was of the sick variety. He took the opportunity during our short walk from the van to the precinct to proposition me by slipping me his number and posting it through a small hole cut out in the back of my Gucci dress – classy.

The offending piece of paper proceeded to scratch and irritate me every time I walked as the shackles were heavy, and the only technique I could find, which would result in me walking in a straight line, was to lift and kick each leg out before I'd take a step, slightly reminiscent of a cart horse.

Kimmi, on the other hand, did not find the time to perfect this technique and proceeded to shuffle along behind me, swaying every now and then from the weight of the shackles, from this side to that.

It was not until we were well inside the precinct that I begin to realise the importance and logic behind the shackling arrangement, which was to safely secure us to a whole host of dangerous female criminals they had picked up during their Manhattan night patrol.

There would be a small metal connecting device between the shackles. This they'd use to clip onto the next person and all 30 of us got shuffled into an overly intimate holding cell after being asked to remove our clothes and replacing them with a prison gown.

Then we had to bend down and cough while a female officer bent over and had a look up your cucci to make sure you were not using it as a holding device to stash you drugs in - an experience I could have done without to put it mildly. However, that was nothing compared to what was in store for us whilst in the cell.

'What's that flapping noise?' questioned Kimmi as we walked to the back of the cell to find a clear patch of floor to crouch down on which, looking around us, seemed like the customary thing to do. I could hear the flapping noise too however, my bigger concern was not to throw up over the both of us, as the smell of piss at this point was overwhelming.

I shrug my shoulders to Kimmi whilst looking around to investigate where this strange noise was coming from. It was almost as if a small bee or little insect were trapped somewhere and struggling to find its way out, but that was impossible of course as this cell was well underground and it would never have survived the transition from the sky to here. But where was it coming from?

Kimmi and I started surveying the area from person to person, body to body to body, as they laid sprawled out on the mats in front of us and there it was: the local crack head no less, with a hole in her nose far bigger than was a socially acceptable size (whatever that was) where the air would come in and filter out through the side, making it flap like a wind tunnel. We both looked at each other in slight revolt but what can you do? We both gripped each other sideways and started to pray for the daylight to come… 'It has to come Kimmi' I told her, 'it will come…'

It was impossible to sleep properly in these conditions but we tried. I shut my eyes for a few moments at a time, only to be jolted awake by someone passing around what smelt like rancid milk and stale jam sandwiches thrown through the bars.

Kimmi and I had not eaten for a good 12 hours but still couldn't bring ourselves to accept their supposedly generous offering, and passed it on to crack head with the flappy nose. She in turn acted as if it were Christmas come early and suddenly sprung to life, making a make-shift picnic for herself on the floor and wolfing down its contents.

It's all about the little things, I thought to myself, too drained in my utterly chaotic brain at this stage to even recognise the irony in this thought. I rolled over onto my side with one eye half on Kimmi and tried to get some sleep… anything to pass the time…

I had no idea how long they had kept us down there for, lying on that rancid floor, but it was long enough, trust me. Long enough for night to become day and the reality of the disgusting yet ridiculous situation to kick in.

Fatigue had pulled a damp cloth over any enthusiasm I could possibly have for anything other than getting my freedom back, that was for sure. Besides, it was not Kimmi and I they really wanted to see nailed for this situation, it was the brains behind the operation they were really gunning for, which I for one had no idea about and as for Kimmi, well at this point I wouldn't like to say.

They called my name, that's all I remembered… They called out my name through the bars of the cell… I slowly rose to my feet, feeling weak and disorientated. *This was it,* I thought to myself, stepping forward through the sea of bodies, but what of Kimmi?

I suddenly stopped. There was no mention of her name, just mine. That was strange I thought. They brought us in together, why would we not leave together or maybe, oh crap! It then dawned on me: she had technically committed a criminal offence, you know, answering the phones and stuff, manning the operation but me, they never really ever had a charge for me, you can't hold someone in a cell indefinitely for bad behaviour.

I knew they had to come for me eventually, but Kimmi? I had no idea what would happen to her.

She squeezed my hand 'Just go babe, I need to sort this one out' she said, almost looking through me.

'But when will I see you?' I asked slightly panicky now. 'What will happen to you?'

She didn't have a chance to answer, the female prison warden had already unbolted the thick metal gates and this was not the place to hang around - they didn't need to call my name twice.

I was handed back my belongings all still in clear white polythene bags and told in no uncertain terms to get loss and never fuck around with anyone in the New York police department again. I took their advice, only stopping off for a cup of tea on the way home and then walking the 10 lonely blocks back to Columbus circus, Douglas and the agency apartment.

Chapter 6

Written whilst listening to 'Here comes the hotstepper' by Ini Kamoze

August 15th 1996, mid-afternoon, British Airways flight.

I was sat three rows from the back gazing at the clouds from my window seat in the aeroplane set for London. They almost had a healing quality to them I thought, as they drifted on by.

Mmhmm... cloud therapy, now there's a new one! Dunno if it would catch on though, too close to Heaven and all that.

Just as well as my reality at this current time was not quite so majestic. In fact, too much to think about.

Also, in the event of a crash, you know, if this aeroplane were to go down, I was probably in the worst possible position as Money always told me: 'If you suffer from engine failure up there always remember, the back goes down first'. *Well, I am properly fucked,* I thought to myself, looking back.

I ordered another drink. Well, what else was there to do thirty thousand feet up in the air when in the event of a crash you had 90% chance of dying? And we wouldn't be landing in London for another - I glanced down at my watch - good 2 hours and I, for one, wanted to be prepared.

After Douglas firmly but politely asked me to leave and Kimmi got the sack from the agency, combined with the whole arrest business, it did seem to take a fair amount of red wine to sooth my nerves these days or that was what I told myself, asking the air hostess for a fresh glass as she went past.

Well, you didn't expect me to fly economy now did you? And anyway the ticket was already bought by banker Marti and it would only have gone to waste! Shame we never actually got to meet properly, Marti and me, but life has a habit of surprising us all and I was sure he'd get over it, just like I had.

Reclining my seat back, I flipped my Jimmy Choo's off - my last remaining pressie from Money. *I wonder what happened to him, people can't just disappear like that? He had to be somewhere.*

That reminded me: must give Mimi a call on my arrival, just out of politeness really. Not that I needed her, I mean, things weren't that bad yet, were they?

In a few hours' time I'd be moving into a new pad. Yes, that's right, straight from the airport in fact. One of Kimmi's old customers from The Hustler Club NYC had kindly lent her the keys to their cousin's place, some penthouse flat just off *The* Edgware Road, no less, and Kimmi thought it to be her duty to help re- house me on my arrival to London as she was directly responsible for the fact I was even here, on this flight.

So I graciously accepted the offer in return for forgetting her error in judgment which led us to that hellish night in the Manhattan precinct. Sounded like a fair deal to me and anyway, these cats weren't even living there.

I'd have the whole place to myself, well, until her impending court case was over with and she could leave NYC for good and until then? The whole place was mine baby! Oh yeah! Let the good times roll!

Edgware Road, for those of you who don't know, is a major road that runs through North-West London, starting from Marble Arch - the more salubrious end where I would be (naturally) - and running up all the way into several North London boroughs.

The area that I would be residing in had always been known for attracting wealthy Arab migrants, the chic Lebanese and, if you're lucky, on a good day, the odd well educated Egyptian no less - quite a cultural melting pot, right in the heart of the city.

How and why Kimmi got the keys to this place was anyone's guess but I just had to go with it for now.

Douglas had advised me to let him and the situation in NY cool down a bit before my return - when that would be God only knew and anyway, something about this new location intrigued me. I was almost looking forward to it, with no agency breathing down my neck and no schedule to adhere to, I could be a free agent, come and go as I pleased, you know, be independent, whatever that meant exactly but it sounded good and I was willing to give it a go at any rate.

'How the hell did you swing this one babe?' remarked Rebel quite visibly impressed as he entered the penthouse style flat, running his hand over the teak detailing of the wood on the Victorian bureau, just off the main living area. 'This is stylish,' he added, 'I have to admit.'

Having only just arrived myself I had no idea of what was here, or what wasn't, so I went to have a look at the content of the fridge and headed to the kitchen for a hopefully, fingers crossed, and… Bingo! We were in luck. *What is it with Middle Eastern men and Cristal champagne?* I thought to myself, removing a bottle of Cristal Rosé from the bottom shelf and then rummaging around the freezer department for some ice, not really quite believing my own luck.

Dark had already located a couple of glasses and was stood ready, waiting for me to pour.

'So you never did tell me what exactly went down in NY babe' Rebel went on in an overly curious manner, 'Kimmi neither… In fact, the both of you are really staying very quiet about the whole shenanigans, whatever they might be, I mean' he continued, 'it can't have been that bad, surely?'

I didn't want to answer him. Bringing it up would have been for me almost as bad as living the whole hellish mess again, and I certainly didn't want to do that.

'Let's talk about it later', I went on, taking a now filled glass from him and hastily sipping on the champers which now was extra cold and frothy due to the ice we'd added, a little trick I'd picked up from Mimi which I'm sure would leave wine buffs or anyone that knew about expensive plonk cold with fear, but it worked for me and that was what counted wasn't it?

Just then the doorbell went and I went to fetch another glass, knowing exactly who it would be.

'Hey you!' trilled Dark bopping into the room with way too much enthusiasm for a normal day and defiantly high on something, that was for sure. I gave her a light peck on the cheek and she removed the spare glass from my hand, picked up the bottle on the table, poured herself a glass and then proceeded to down it in one, appreciatively.

'Oh yeah! That's what I'm talking about, just what I needed' she said, placing the empty glass down on the table and letting out I quaint little belch.

'So, what's new?' she went on, 'Where's Kimmi?'

Rebel looked to me and I back to him, both acknowledging that giving Dark any information that could be misrepresented in any form or used for malicious gossip would be the death sentence for the people involved i.e. myself and Kimmi. Dark had the habit of broadcasting to people even the most private information about one's lives faster than the world service and this, this time, needed to be under wraps and self-contained for as long as humanly possible.

'She got detained in NY' I finally answered after a long gap in conversation, 'but she'll be over soon.' I added.

'Yes' agreed Rebel, 'I'm sure it won't be long before she sorts her visa requirements out' he said, taking a quick swig of his champers and giving me a knowing look. Thankfully Dark didn't seem to twig anything and happily accepted my offer of a refill; distraction by champagne… always a good ploy.

I looked at the time, it was coming up to 5 p.m., hardly a late hour, but jet lag combined with excess tiredness, then a drop of champagne added in the mix, and you had complete meltdown. I felt my legs wobble and a heaviness in my chest.

'I'm just going to lay down a bit guys' I said by mean of explanation and took myself off to the bedroom with barely enough energy to get undressed. I flopped down on the bed. 'Make yourselves at home!' I managed to blurt out just before my head hit the pillow. *I'm sure they will* I thought to myself curling my legs up into a fetal position and drifting off into a peaceful uninterrupted sleep to the gentle murmur of traffic heading down the Edgware road .

Something jolted me out of my sleep and I momentarily totally forgot where I was. What the fuck? I looked around me - which wasn't helpful as I was in 80% darkness at least - I found a bedside lamp and switched it on looking at the time on some sort of digital alarm clock by the bed: 2.30 a.m. Marvelous. What to do now?

Hearing no noise or signs of life coming from the main living area meant Rebel and Dark must have let themselves out. They probably ran out of booze, I mused, and headed to the kitchen to fetch myself a glass of water, suddenly feeling alone and slightly lost. *Christ it's cold!* I thought to myself opening up what looked like an airing cupboard and finding a blanket to drape around me. This was due to an over-zealous aircon system which I just couldn't seem to turn down.

I then located my phone which had been long since abandoned and tossed down carelessly between the cushions on the sofa. I switched it on... 27 new messages it read... *How is this so?* I was thinking... Only 2 bloody people knew I was back. *Oh fuck! I hope no one has died!* I suddenly flung into a panic, scrolling through the messages one by one, looking for numbers relating to the countryside, the family dialing code but no, these were all foreign numbers: a couple of international dialing codes and long strange mobiles numbers. Nothing familiar at all.

I opened the first: 'I'll be with you for 3 a.m.' it read, 'Keep your phone on, I have no keys'. What the hell? Who could this… Then I twigged: it had to be Kimmi, she must have jumped her court date which wasn't a smart move, but nothing I could do about it as it sounded like she was on her way. I didn't know if I was happy or disappointed.

It was only Money who would call me from all sorts of strange numbers, international dialing codes and stuff, but why I was even thinking about this I didn't know. Money was long gone, he didn't even have this number, not to mention the fact I didn't think I had any real feelings for him whatsoever. *Why do I keep going over it? It was all about the money* I kept telling myself, *I'm just remembering it wrongly*. I needed him and he helped me, simple. I had also since worked out, I didn't really need him, or anyone for that matter. All I needed was me and a fat wallet, that was it. 'Don't expect anything from anyone', that was my motto. That's how it was. That was the way forward.

Just then I heard a taxi draw up outside. That had to be her I thought, going to the window; it was a black cab, I could hear it, they were noisy.

Kimmi was talking or haggling should I say with the driver. She didn't have enough money. *Oh for Christ's sake!* She was trying to get around him. It was not working. I grabbed my shoes from the bedroom, a fifty pound note I found in one of the drawers and headed downstairs into the cool night breeze.

'Look love' went on the cabbie, 'I picked you up all the way from Heathrow; 20 quid ain't gonna cover it, I need 50 at least.' Kimmi started pouting and playing with her hair.

I was way too cold and tired for this nonsense, I leaned in to the front of the cab and paid the driver, taking the 20 quid from his hands and replacing it with the 50 pound note. 'We're out of here.' I instructed Kimmi, helping her with her bags out the back.

'Good riddance!' shouted the Cockney cabbie, slapping the door behind us, 'and next time, make sure you've got the correct fare!' and with that he sped off.

'What's his problem?' demanded Kimmi, hands on hips. 'Some people!' she added without any detection of irony.

I couldn't be bothered to talk at this point and silently helped her get her bags inside. We were both absolutely exhausted and once inside, jumped into the double bed fully clothed to beat the relentless cold.

'Got any slippers?' asked Kimmi with her hand out in my direction.

'No I don't' I responded. 'And don't ask me again, you don't need them.' I added, pulling up the duvet cover to around our ears, in the hope we would both drift off to sleep. 'Good night Kimstar'.

'Goodnight English' she replied sounding just like Douglas used to. We both started to chuckle, I turned off the light and it was back to darkness once more.

Something that I had found to be true of Kimmi and something I'm sure she would never admit was that when it comes to arrangements, you know, such as this, there were always highly important details she just happened to neglect to mention, these details usually had a habit of impacting on people's lives, namely mine.

Next morning, 9.45 a.m., still Edgware Road.

'Oh I need a croissant' remarked Kimmi as we made our way down the Edgware Road looking for a suitable place to have some form of breakfast.

That could be ambitious I thought to myself as all we seemed to pass were Middle Eastern style cafés with outside chairs and tables filled with middle-aged men brandishing hub ali bubbling pipes, more commonly known as hookah.

However the coffee did smell good and there were some women sitting on tables just inside near the counter. We decided to give it a go, went in, sat down and ordered two very strong coffees accompanied by some form of pastries.

'Mmhmm!' remarked Kimmi, 'Who needs the French? These are sooo good!'

I couldn't have agreed more and we ordered two more cakes whilst enjoying the smell of the apple tobacco being smoked by some guys outside as it wafted through the open doors of the café.

Then Kimmi started to talk. I should have expected this conversation to come but like always, I just didn't see it coming.

'So you know, Waffi' she said.

'No, Waffi who?' I replied not having a clue who she was on about.

'You know my friend's cousin who owns the flat we're staying in'.

'Oh yes' I replied skeptically, 'What about him?'

'Well,' she continued, 'He's due to be in London later on tonight and I sort of said that we'd go out to dinner with him.'

'Oh fucking brilliant! I replied, 'Another fucked up plan waiting to happen, what else have you promised him?'

'Oh nothing, nothing', replied Kimmi, 'He just said he'd like to meet you, that's all. Oh come on, one dinner's not going to hurt you and anyway, what else are you going to do this evening?'

'Oh I'll find something to do Kimstar, trust me on that one and anyway, that's not the point Kimmi,' I responded, 'I just don't want you making these plans for me all the time, that's all. I just want to be uncomplicated for a while.'

'Ok', said Kimmi solemnly, 'I'll just go on my own then and if you change your mind we'll be in a restaurant on the Gloucester Road ok?'

'Ok' I said, paying the bill, 'you just do that.' We got up and left the café.

Back at the apartment.

She had only been gone an hour or so but already I was at a loose end. I really wanted to call Mimi, I'd missed her in a strange perverse sort of a way. However that really wasn't my main goal in making contact it was more about what happened to Money and my lack of it that bothered me.

I went to the kitchen and fetched the last remaining bottle of champers. *Thanks Waffi or whatever the hell your name is* I thought to myself, *hope you and Kim star have a lovely time this evening and this is to you!* I made a lonely toast and knocked back a glass Darkstar fashion all in one. Than the next. Than the next, Dutch courage and all that as I didn't know quite how Mimi would receive my phone call. We hadn't left it on the best of terms and... *Oh fuck it!* I thought to myself and dialled the number.

I just had time to locate a Marlboro from my bag, sparked it up and then a voice answered however it definitely wasn't Mimi's. In fact I had no idea whose voice it was but it looked like I was just about to find out.

'Oh hi!' I said stumbling over my words, 'I'm looking for Mimi, you don't by any chance have any idea where I can find her do you?'

There came a long pause... 'And this is?' came the woman's voice on the other end, not wanting to give too much away.

'Oh, an old friend of hers' I said, 'She introduced me to someone.'

'Oh I see.' said the lady 'Well she is still in that game, you know' she paused again 'of introductions but I'm afraid she's moved abroad now and won't be back for some time.'

'Oh that's a shame' I said disappointed. 'I wanted to ask her...'

She stopped me there 'Look my puppet' she said, 'You sound young, are you very young?' she asked hopefully.

'Well,' I went on, 'I'm not quite twenty yet, is that young?' I asked her back.

'Yes, yes it is darling so what I suggest is this: I'll pass on a message to Mimi that you called and in the meantime, why don't you pop along to the Met Bar and meet a couple of friends of mine. I'm sure you're quite attractive,' she added with a giggle, 'Mimi only has attractive friends'.

'Who am I meeting?' I asked in bewilderment.

'Well,' she went on, 'His name is Serge, he's from a very wealthy Mexican family and he's over here sightseeing for a few days with a pal, also male. They are both nineteen years old and would love some company. I don't know who to call as Mimi has her address book away with her, so if you fancy popping down there be my guest.'

I stopped and thought for a moment… What I thought I was needing was an evening of solitude and contemplation however that really wasn't helping matters. What I needed was to get out of this strange Edgware Road flat before I went stir crazy and anyway, maybe if I did this, maybe I could get back in Mimi's good books again and she'd tell me where Money was, if I wanted to know, of course, it was an option. And after a slight hesitation, I agreed to go.

It was nearing 9 p.m. by the time I got to the bar and I was already 3 sheets to the wind due to the champers I'd been quaffing back in Edgware Road. I used the remaining 20 pound note I had got from Kimmi the previous evening to pay the cab from Edgware Road to Park Lane where the bar was and got the taxi to drop me off directly outside the entrance, as the heels I'd decided to wear where far too high to walk any distance in, not to mention the cold lapping at my feet.

Mimi's friend, let's call her Patricia, informed me they'd be waiting for me at the bar, so that was exactly where I headed as it was far too expensive in there for me to by my own drinks. Furthermore, I didn't even think I had ever bought myself any of my own drinks before, I'd always been taken and I was certainly not going to break the habit of a life time for these punks, no way!

I spied someone that looked suspiciously like it could be them out the corner of my eye while I bopped through the glass revolving doors. Thank God it was a Tuesday evening and there were hardly any people in there as this whole process could have been confusing.

I took up a bar stool and propped myself up, highly visible in the middle of the bar, ordered a glass of champagne and instructed the bar man that the short young looking guy at the far end of the bar was paying for my drink along with his equally short friend in the pink shirt.

'Ok honey,' said the bar man with a slight smile, 'I'll just go over and tell them shall I?'

'As you wish.' I replied in my mock foreign accent suddenly feeling in the mood to cause some trouble.

I saw them talk with the bar man, look over at me, then pay for my drink. I knew it was them and they in turn knew it was me. A smile spread across the not so short one's face, a face that only a mother could have loved. He walked over to me followed by the very short one in the pink.

'Hello,' I said to the first one ignoring the hand he had out stretched for me to shake, to go in and give him a kiss, a big one on the mouth. He was taken aback but I continued 'You must be Serge' I said with a smile, 'and this must be your sidekick.' I added, giving his friend a firm hand shake.

The friend was of a nervous disposition and had a constant twitch of the left eye. *Christ, this is gonna be a long evening!* I thought to myself, *Where the fuck is Kimmi when you need her!*

'Look' I said to Serge, leading them away from the bar and onto an empty alcove near the back, 'why don't I give my friend a ding and see what she's doing, that way you and I can chat without your friend here getting fed up. What do you say?' I added, hopeful.

'Hmm' replied Serge looking slightly less nervous of me now. 'Ok' he added sitting down next to me.

I was just about to ring Kimmi when I saw a waiter passing by us. I made a nod to grab his attention. *Good he's coming over.* I cleared my throat 'We'd like some champagne please' I told him looking at Serge. Serge gave me the nod in agreement and I went ahead and ordered. 'We'll have one bottle of Cristal and...' I paused for a second 'and a Dom Perignon.' - stick to the classics - then sent a message to Kimmi in the hope she was having a shit evening with what's his face and wanted to change her plans.

Bingo! Kimmi rocked up to the bar precisely 20 mins later looking very pleased with herself. She was drunk and in a silly mood. *Good that makes two of us* I thought to myself and made a space for her to plonk her drunken arse down next to mine.

'So you, what ever happened to prince Waffi? How did you get out of that one?' I asked laughing, giving her some champers, not that she needed any more but anyway.

'Well' she went on, 'the guy's a complete prick. In fact I left him in the restaurant so when you called it was perfect timing.'

'Ok' I said sobering up slightly as the realisation suddenly hit me that one of us had to keep this guy sweet as we were staying in his place. 'Soooo how did you leave it?' I asked 'And what was exactly wrong with him?'

'Well,' said Kimmi taking a large slurp of champagne 'For starters he was annoyed I didn't bring you.'

'Ok' I replied feeling slightly guilty (but not too much obviously), 'What else?'

'Well,' she continued 'he also wanted to talk about the size and shapes of my lady parts whilst in the restaurant.'

'Oh no!' I added trying not to laugh,

'Yes,' she continued, 'it really started to put me off my prawns. Then by the time we had reached our main course that topic had moved on to rear entry'.

'What?' I added.

'You know,' she went on, 'Sex up the bum'.

'Oh no!' I said again, 'He could have at least waited until you got to pudding!' I now sniggered.

Kimmi: 'It was so inconsiderate, not to mention annoying!'

'I bet,' I added, 'so how did you get out of it?'

'Well,' she went on, 'when you sent that message I said you'd had some kind of emergency and I'd have to come now.'

'Well sounds credible.' I said. 'And, so, how did you leave it?' I asked hoping she'd left us with options at least?

Kimmi took a long slow sip of champagne and proceeded to change the subject. 'So these guys are from Mexico right?'

'Kimmmmmiiii!!!' I said exasperated now, 'Please, tell me we don't have to leave the apartment, please?' I added hopeful but already half-knowing the answer.

'Hmm well,' she went on, 'Not today' downing her champagne and filling it up again.

'When?' I asked, putting my hand over the glass before she had a chance to drink it. She looked me in the eye nervously.

'Just tell me.' I said, looking at her straight back.

'Friday' she finally replied head in hands.

I couldn't speak for a moment or two, just letting it sink in. I picked up her glass of champagne I'd been stopping her from drinking and downed it in one, then decided to speak: 'Kimmmmi!!!' I finally responded with a yell lauder than I intended, 'What the fuck are we gonna do?!'

'I dunno' she responded suddenly looking into the eyes of Serge's twitting faced friend, swirling her hair and pushing her leg up to his underneath the table.

Oh no! I thought to myself. *Not this, it can't have come to this.*

I suddenly felt like I was in the distance watching the thing unravel almost in slow motion. So she purred to him right up in his right ear, left hand resting on his inner thigh, 'We ain't never been to Mexico ya know'…

In transit, 5.45 p.m.

'Oh, goin loco down in Acapulco… if you stay too long… yes you'll be goin loco la la Acapulco, the magic down there is so strong… oh ya…' sang Kimmi.

'Kimstar,' I interrupted her, 'I hate to break it to you but firstly that's a bullshit song and secondly Mexico City, where we're going, is nowhere near fucking Acapulco.' *At least I don't think it is.*

I was now trying to read the map I found behind the seat at the back of the aeroplane. *Now let's have a closer look…* Ok, well, she did have a point, they did both look to be in the same proximity on the map but I had never been one to read maps. However I'd hazard at a guess they were around a few hours of each other by car (could be wrong). Anyway… what did it say… *oh here we go*: 'before Cancun and Itapúa, Acapulco was Mexico's original party town with stunning yellow beaches and 24 hour nightlife' *Alright!*

So, let's have a look at Mexico City: 'Organised chaos rules in this high-octane megalopolis.' *Hmm, sounds like our kind of place...* I glanced around at the two seats behind.

Serge's seat was reclined right back which was causing him to sleep with his mouth wide open - I'd seen more attractive sights, trust me. Twitchy, next to him, was doing what he did best, yes you guessed it, twitching. I didn't know whether it had been made worse by the altitude but he looked very uncomfortable indeed.

Kimmi, in true Kimmi style, was completely oblivious to anything going on around her that wasn't directly benefiting her, so the only person that had her undivided attention right now was the air stewardess who happened to be bringing her the 3rd Pina Colada of that flight so far (we'd only been in the air 1 hour 20 minutes). But anyway, *Thank God for business class!* as I stretched out to assume a pose not dissimilar to Serge's for the rest of the flight.

My mind started to wander off into a dreamlike state as minutes turned to hours and I slowly dosed off... I was walking through rain forests and along tropical beaches, I was surrounded by splashing fountains as the palm fronted beaches disappeared from my view - but it then dawned on me it was not in fact Mexico I was dreaming... more like the Congo...

The first thing to strike me when we landed in this new country was how it was a city of contrasts. While the poor get poorer and more visibly poor, the rich get richer and more visibly corrupt but whom was I to judge, the place had had its fair share of turbulent past with some violent surprises thrown into the mix.

We were immediately met by some heavy looking body guards at arrivals - something that Serge always apparently travels with - however they brought me little to no comfort, the opposite in fact. They led us out the front of the airport and into a waiting, blacked out bulletproof car. Standard procedure I was told for people around here with money.

The driver of the blackout Merc we were about to get into had the same feeling of resentment and moroseness to him as the security did. However I convinced myself that it was just my currently unhappy frame of mind telling me this and there really was no need for my nervousness of thought.

Serge who was sat to the left of the driver in the front seat must have noticed my unease and swivelled round in his chair to face me: 'Look' he said taking my hand in his, 'I understand' he went on 'that this is a lot of information for you two girls to take in, first time in Mexico and all that.'

Kimmi looked to me and I back to Kimmi. 'Yes' we both said in agreement.

'But look,' he went on 'We didn't bring you here to kill you ok? I mean Christ, I like you, I like you both' he added. 'Now my parents are away from the house for the next few days and we have the run of things. You'll like it, trust me.'

We both then visibly started to relax. 'It'll be all right' said Kimmi turning to me in a low voice, 'Just treat it as a vacation' she added. 'Play our cards right, we may even make it down to Acapulco, ok English?'

'Ok Kimmi' I replied, taking in the sights out the window as day began to turn to dusk.

We were high up in the northern Mexican city hills now with views of the valley below....

The Cartel's Mansion, 9.45 p.m.

We pulled up to some sort of mansion house neatly nestled behind some strong yet sleek looking cast iron gates. The gates were tall and black and attached to a very high wall that ran around the whole length of the property.

Electronically yet slowly the gates began to open, revealing one of the biggest and most beautiful mansion houses I thought I'd ever seen before and I'd seen a few. Forget Hugh Hefner baby, this was the real deal! In fact I'd never seen Kimmi look so animated about anything before in our whole little tiny lives.

'This is off the hook' she whispered to me. 'Twitch or no twitch baby, I am never leaving this pad' and I believed her for we had certainly hit the jackpot this time with these two punks, that was for sure. For this place was something of legends, louche yet luxuriously over the top with gold leafed furniture of thrown-like proportions, slightly hard to describe style wise but think 'opulence' mixed with Scarface and we get a pretty good visual. This was untouchably a shady world of extremes we had just walked into - with the desire for sophistication which translated in a slight tackiness. However they'd created something, that was for sure.

Wouldn't like to speculate what Serge's parents did for a living but I was sure we could safely say they were involved in the import-export trade. We walked through the grand entrance lobby that led off to the kitchen. There was a marble topped bar towards the end of the kitchen towards which Serge headed to fix us all a large whisky and coke, no ice.

He flipped a switch from behind the bar to reveal a flood lit swimming pool, designed in the shape of a massive great guitar. It was so large it ran almost half the length of the property. *I'll test that out tomorrow!* I thought to myself turning to Kimmi, watching her eyes widen with excitement.

Serge then got one of the staff to show us to our rooms, Kimmi's to be on the top floor opposite mine. It was a five storey palace and just to climb that many stairs really took it out of you. However much I wanted to stay up and investigate this place, it would have to wait as my body was telling me otherwise.

My room looked over the guitar shaped swimming pool with views stretching high up into the northern mountains. I then pulled a cord to close off the blinds and moved over to the bed where I pulled back layers of the finest Egyptian cotton sheets, the type that Money always slept under. I got undressed and crawled into the bed, the softness almost overwhelming me with comfort and I was asleep within minutes.

Wow! So fucking loud! I opened my eyes, got up and followed the sound of music. I couldn't even make out exactly what music it was they were playing, not through lack of volume of course but mainly because of the distortion.

The other form of unwanted noise was coming from Kimmi who was sat straddling Twitchy's shoulders in a Union Jack bikini as she jumped around the pool. This was much to the delight of Serge and his merry group of friends who looked as though they were on their third or fourth cocktail each at least, jumping around the pool side and just generally making tits of themselves.

Funnily enough I had no inclination to join them right now, no, I'd rather have a snoop around this place and find out what was really going down there, I mean, some liberal parents he must have, going away and leaving this lot to party in a pad like this. I took another glance at the morons out of the window, who were all in the pool by then, just to reaffirm my opinions of proceedings. Yep, there was no doubt about it, the blind were leading the blind, that was for sure.

I really wanted to go downstairs and make myself some tea but this would have drawn too much attention to the fact I was awake and Serge would be onto me to join them. No, whatever I was doing, it needed to be now, and quickly too. I flung some clothes out of the one bag I had brought with me and hurriedly put them on. They were creased and crinkled but I didn't care, we were in Mexico, who gave a shit.

I sneaked out the bedroom and crept down the hallway, padding along in my bare feet. I came across some sort of office to the left of me, all in dark wood panels on the wall. I took a good look around to make sure the coast was clear then darted in there, quickly closing the door behind me. There was some sort of desk to the middle of the room so I made for that, my hands shaking as I went to open the top drawer. But before I did so I spied a big bag of white powder just sitting on the floor near the foot of the desk. *It can't be, that can't be dusty showbiz* (coke) *there's too much of it*.

I took the bag up to my nose and took a big sniff - you know for a mini toxicology report - it took a few moments to kick in so, I put my finger in to taste, just to be sure. *Fuck that was strong! Yes, definitely coke.* I put the bag down where I found it and went back to the desk, not quite anticipating what I would find there...

I opened the drawer slowly... there were several boxes of prescription pills and some liquids. I then slid my hand to the back of the drawer to find a big bundle of cash, and next to the cash a fucking Beretta pistol and several cases for Glock pistols. I froze. This was too much information! I expected to find something but not this, this was out of my league this stuff, a league I'd prefer not to be in, Kimmi neither.

We needed to make our excuses and leave, sooner rather than later. Running to the nearest window I opened it and took a look out - good, all still in the pool. In a dead panic I flicked on the TV and found CNN.

'The Mexican drug war is an ongoing armed conflict' the news reader reported, 'Rival drug cartels fight one another for regional control... the Mexican government has claimed that their primary focus is on dismantling the powerful drug cartels... although Mexican drug cartels or drug trafficking organisations have existed for several decades, they have become more powerful since the demise of the opposition. Benzoylmethylecgonine otherwise known as cocaine is obtained from the leaves of the coco plant. When taken in high quantities, it can cause extreme anxiety and complete paranoia...' *Oh bloody hell! They have brought us here to kill us, I know it!*

I popped downstairs and tried to go on like nothing had happened, making some tea, which was not as easy as it sounded after you'd seen all that. Images kept popping into my head of severed horses heads in my bed, spreading blood all over those beautiful Egyptian sheets. I planned to get us out of there as quickly as humanly possible.

Just then Serge walked into the kitchen brandishing a champagne glass that was almost definitely for me. 'Thank you sweetie' I said taking it from him, 'but I think I'll finish my tea first' and I rested it down on the table next to the tray. I caught my hand shaking as I did this, *Fuck this isn't good* I thought to myself sipping my tea slowly.

Serge came and sat next to me, pulling up a chair. 'I think you're nervous of me' he said with a smile looking into my face.

Well of course I am!

Just then Kimmi flew into the kitchen brandishing two glasses and looking for some ice. He got up to leave (Serge), *Thank God for that!* I'm saying in my mind.

'Kimmi,' I hissed in a hushed whisper 'We have to get out of here, as soon as possible!' I added, grabbing at her arm. 'These guys, Serge and the other two Pedro and Salvatore or whatever the hell their names are, are all part of a longstanding, intricate and elaborate conspiracy plot to kidnap and murder us. How could we have not seen it coming I don't know!' I added in total panic.

Kimmi looked at me with worry and concern. 'English,' she went on in a tentative tone, 'I really hope you ain't been sniffing that gear that Serge has got, it'll make you a crazy paranoid fool' she added.

'No Kimmi I'm serious' I said, 'We have to get out of here and anyway,' I went on 'it's not the coke,' I said, half trying to convince myself at this point, 'the coke only boosted my enormous analytical abilities to find this conspiracy out!' I added frantically.

She stared back at me in disbelief, hands on hips, trying not to laugh.

'Yes.' I added again, thoroughly unconvincingly, 'That's why Sherlock Holmes used to smoke so much of it, it boosted his analytical skills enormously too! It's the magic dust of perception Kimmi. It helps you know exactly what's going on.'

'Look, English' Kimmi said still trying not to laugh and making her way towards the door, 'If you wanna leave this place, fine, ok, we'll leave but spare me the bullshit ok?' And with that she walked out the double patio doors and jumped back into the pool.

I don't care what she thinks I thought to myself, *these punks were in an elaborate plot to kill us and I for one would make damn sure it wasn't going to happen.*

The beauty parlour.

The next day Serge and his mate took us down to some sort of beauty parlour - *a perfect criminal hideout* I thought to myself. Every single thing in the place was pink, they had pink walls, pink blinds, pink wash basins, pink chair and pink towels for the hair.

'This place is bizarre' remarked Kimmi as we entered the salon. I couldn't have agreed with her more as I ran my hand along the pink wall papered corridor... What the hell was this lady thinking of painting it this colour?

'This bitch must be on some seriously hard core drugs' Kimmi added laughing and looking in my direction which I didn't find funny at all, still thinking they were in some sort of elaborate kidnap plot.

'Be careful' I whispered, 'we don't know how good their English is' *Plus they might try to kill us right here!* I wanted to add but managed to refrain from saying it, even though I thought it all the same.

They sat us down on two chairs one next to each other. We then managed to use mime and sign language to convey what we wanted done without being killed. That was quite successful.

They got straight to work on the hair (the murderer accomplices) whilst a masseuse started to work on our necks and shoulders; she gently slid my top down my arms and dispenses the oil from her hands over my skin at the top of my spine, rubbing it rhythmically.

I wanted to close my eyes and switch off, letting the thoughts in my mind run like a river to the shore I imagined lapping at my toes. The tension drained from my body and I breathed deeply, not wanting to move or speak. I looked to Kimmi who was in an equally blissed out state.

'I need to talk to you' I said, straining my neck over in order to see her under a mass of blond hair. 'It's important.'

She looked up with a smile 'The only thing missing is a cocktail' she added, looking in the owner's direction.

'I'm sure she could arrange it' I added with a gulp… 'And here's the problem…' I started from the beginning, explaining to Kimmi what I had seen and expressing my undoubted fears. She listened, surprisingly attentively, probably sensing the severity of the situation or just trying to pacify me, one or the other.

'So how do we get out of this fucking place?' she whispered

looking annoyed.

'Look,' I went on, 'after dinner today, Serge is having people over to the house. You can bet your arse on the fact they'll be drinking and partying hard, this is when we make our move. Remember the body guard?' I said, 'The one that liked you' I added, 'the one by the swimming pool when you were in the pool?'

'Yes' she replied.

'Well' I said, 'he doubles up as a driver for them sometimes, so what we do is we wait till much later on, you know, when they're all on the old dusty showbiz and stuff, you take him aside and talk him into driving us to the airport. Do whatever it takes ok? We'll then leave in the middle of the night. Then bamm, we're gone ok?'

'And how are we gonna fly on these tickets?' she added, 'The departure date on them is not till next week.'

'Once at the airport' I said, 'You call that plastic surgeon friend of yours, you know Dr. Rock or whatever the fuck his name is and you tell him we need to change our flights due to some medical emergency we might die of. That way, he contacts the airline on our behalf, and we won't need to pay any excess, ok?'

'Ok, English' she replied in mock seriousness, 'this better work' she added looking at me again.

'It will Kimmi,' I replied, 'just chill.' I added, giving her leg a squeeze. 'It'll all work out fine, I promise.' And with that I took a Marlboro out my bag in preparation to light up as soon as the lady had finished my hair for at this moment, I needed it. Fucking hell, I needed it.

I can't tell you much about the restaurant other than there were plants everywhere and all the people dining seemed to be wearing those ridiculously massive, brightly coloured Mexican hats - perfect place to hide a gun I thought - and what tits they all looked was an afterthought however. After about my third Sambuca, I didn't much care. Serge was on good form telling stories and generally entertaining the group, Twitchy even looked relaxed too, sat next to Kimmi who after our mammoth beauty salon afternoon looked absolutely glowingly radiant.

There were a good few other people with us who were pleasant enough. However, getting to know them required more effort than I was prepared to put in and anyway, my criminal knowledge was minimal - better to stick to what you know. So I chatted to Serge and Twitchy about alcoholic beverages and how best to consume them.

As the evening rolled on I started to slow down on the drinking as opposed to speeding up. If we had any hope in hell of getting away that evening I'd have to keep it together and leave the getting wrecked till we got on the plane, if we even made it on there that is. It was touch and go.

Food came and went and the drinks flowed. My Dolce and Gabbana dress, courtesy of Money some time back, came in handy however. It was drawing more attention to me than I had hoped, which left me no breathing space to collect our plan together or even talk to Kimmi who also had her fair share of attention, wanted or otherwise.

Amazingly she had stuck to her side of the plan and made her moves towards security/driver man who couldn't believe his luck by the look of things as her sporadic bouts of attention towards him left him fawning like a love sick puppy dizzy with excitement and playfulness.

It was nearing 1 p.m. now and the journey from the restaurant to the car to the house seemed like an especially long and drawn out process. My legs dragging like lead preempting the pain that was to follow in my head, unfortunate consequences of Sambuca on an empty stomach. Could have done with some of Mexico's finest export, however there is always a price to pay for everything and I thought I'd give it a miss this evening.

Just as predicted the party got cranked to another level once we got back to the house with people dispersing in all directions, hungry for music, laughter and artificial stimulation of any kind. With Serge still hot on my tail I needed to wait until he was at least inebriated enough not to notice I was not there, giving it an hour or so I reckoned. I glanced at my watch then headed out towards the pool area to smoke and be alone. Wow, what a depressive mood I found myself in... *The moon is too bright tonight* I found myself thinking as I looked to the heavens, *Get me out of here...*

I dipped my toe into the over-chlorinated water of the pool, testing the temperature, which was warm. Shame I didn't have time for one last swim, I thought as I left the pool area and headed upstairs to one of the many bedrooms as that seemed to be where the party had relocated to. I tentatively pushed open the first bedroom door, a bedroom if I was not mistaken that didn't actually belong to anyone, just a spare. There was music playing gently in the background and the distinctive smell of someone smoking cannabis filled the air but that was nothing unusual.

In the other room, if my eyes were not deceiving me, laid out on the floor were various guns, some with their Glocks out to show there was no ammo in them and some closed up so there was no way to tell whether they'd be ready to shoot or not. Conducting proceedings was Serge.

Serge sat in the middle, gun in hand, playfully pretending to shoot at the wall. His crew of merry gatherers Pedro, Twitchy and the other one were sat, egging him on quite willing I was sure to have a full on shooting party, running around the mansion as a bunch of gun touting idiots firing at any one or anything that took their interest.

I'd seen enough. I exited the room as slowly and as carefully as I had entered, being careful not to draw attention to myself as I lightly closed the door behind me. I rushed downstairs to find a nervous but prepared looking Kimmi who was as willing to leave now as I was, paronoid delusions or not.

With our bags packed waiting to leave out the back door, the driver she'd been working on all evening sat in the blacked out Merc waiting for us to get in and depart. I looked at my watch, 2 a.m. bang on schedule. We dived out the back exit of the house not looking back and straight into the Merc.

'The airport babe' said Kimmi to the man driving, giving him a gentle tap on the shoulder. He seemed to understand her well enough and that was it, we left the house, Serge, Twitchy and their lunatic friends behind all in the dead of the night.

The Mexican dream was over, that was for sure.

Chapter 7

Written whilst listening to 'Bittersweet Symphony' by The Verve

September 1996, mid-afternoon, Sloane Square, London.

As the days had slowly turned to nights and weeks into months of the year since I had been back, London and I had reacquainted ourselves with each other once more in a more civilised manner this time.

For how long? I hear you ask. Well that remained to be seen but for now I had finally managed to establish some kind of routine, one which more or less worked.

The new agency I had just off Kings Road were being very accommodating for now (they found me a flat at least) and I had also let them know that on no uncertain terms would I get up for any appointments before 11 a.m. due to my very taxing evening job (yes, a complete lie).

With Kimmi back in the States and Mimi still not around these days I seemed to have steered clear of complications. Rebel and Darkstar preferred the bohemia of West London to these Chelsea, Sloane areas so I had little to no distractions - can't be a bad thing I hear you say - however a girl still needs her fair share of fun as the days come and go and the seasons change.

One cold wet wintery afternoon I got a call from some silly little idiot man I'd met in the South of France, what seemed a long time ago. He'd given me a lift home once from a party on the back of his equally silly moped, bright pink in colour and not cool for anyone to ride around on with even half an inch of street cred. He even made me wear the silly fucking helmet that went with it. *Give me a break please!* I thought to myself, but you always get one cuckoo I s'pose.

Anyway, I managed to get back ok, he dropped me off, took my number and I'd never heard from him since. Why he was calling me now was anyone's guess but it seemed I was just about to find out.

'Hey ma Chérie!' he went on in a sort of French accent, more manufactured than authentic, but who knows, anyway 'Vwat are you doing next week?' he questioned, 'I have a dinner' he said, 'I'd really like you to come, lots of interesting people, you would love it my Chérie amour. It's at a very pretty restaurant, not far from Hyde Park. There will be no scooter ok?' he added, 'A very classy evening. What do you say?'

'Oh how thoughtful!' I said, but really having no intention of going to the dinner. 'We shall see' I added, just wanting to get him off the phone, 'Just send me the details I'll let you know.'

'Ok my Chérie' he replied 'Bye for now, I am going now, I have a meeting.'

'Oh don't let me keep you.' I answered, 'Bye and see you soon!'

Wow! I thought putting the phone down, *what a little weirdo creep.*

One week later...

Oh come on, this is a fucking joke! I then opened up the window and hollered out at the silly imitation French man: 'I thought you said no moped?' I yelled. 'What in Jesus's name is that?' I added, gesturing towards the lame looking pink bike. 'It cannot be mistaken for anything else.' I added. 'It is a bright pink scooter, no mistake'.

He hesitated and then came back with 'I secretly thought you liked it,' smiling to himself, 'everyone else does.' he added.

'Well, everyone else is lying to you,' I shot back, 'and I'd be lying to you now if I said that I really wanted to get on the back of that stupid little moped of yours coz I really don't!' I added. 'But you're here now and if you pick me up some Marlboro Lights on the way, I'll come.' I said.

'Ok,' he replied shouting up to me, 'that's a deal!' So I grabbed my coat from the kitchen table, drained the last from the bottle left on the sideboard and made my way downstairs to the midget and his moped.

The restaurant turned out to be Momo's in Kensington, one of my favourites no less.

I found myself a little wobbly on my feet as we entered. I put it down to the traumatic wind resistance travelling on the back of that moped thing but could have easily been down to the wine I'd consumed prior to leaving the flat.

We arrived at the restaurant in good time. Moped driving Midget managed to sum up the brain power to find me the nearest chair on the table we were approaching at the far back of the restaurant and pulled it out for me to sit down on. 'Thank you' I said helping myself to some water that had been left for us in a jug on the far left side of the table.

To the right of me sat some annoying blonde chick with an ego bigger than the room which was quite large to begin with.

To the left of me sat some guy that claimed to be in motor racing but from the looks of things I'd definitely say that he had more age than experiences to look forward to. He was in deep conversation with the blonde girl and I found their English public school accents deeply irritating - *this is going to be a long evening* I thought to myself... Moped Midget then sat down in the chair left side of the blonde girl.

I scanned the remaining tables to see if there was anyone else worth talking to besides these reprobates. There was a girl at the far end that kept catching my eye as if to say we knew each other but I just couldn't think for the life of me where I recognised her face from. It would come to me I was sure, and started to pour some white wine enthusiastically into the nearest glass to me, a chardonnay, hmm not bad I thought taking a big swig.

Now what could I do to liven things up a little... everyone else's glasses were half-empty... well that was no good... I got the wine list and ordered as if we were all gonna die tomorrow, or as if we were on a night out in Beirut.

Two bottles of red, two of white and enough champers to drown a small cricket team. *That should do it* I thought rubbing my hands together. I then got up, still unsteady, and went to the loo.

On my return I couldn't help but notice the girl I thought I'd recognised, the one that had been sat at the other end of the table, had now moved round and positioned herself neatly between the blonde girl and Mr motor racing directly opposite my position on the table. Hmm, let's hope she doesn't start banging on about money or politics - two slightly difficult subjects for me when the only real money I ever had almost always belonged to other people and the only opinions I ever liked had always been my own.

And then it dawned on me who the girl was that had just sat down opposite me. I could spot that quick witted bitch like wit anywhere: that was coke head Kelly from the Ladbroke Grove agency apartment. The one Pattie, my old booker, had asked to leave all that time back after I got falsely blamed for raiding the payphone system while Kelly got out of her mind on coke. *Old habits die hard* I thought to myself as I saw her discreetly snuffle something up her nose from a vile she kept hidden just underneath the table.

'Kelly,' I said walking up to her with a knowing smile, 'how the hell are you?' She is momentarily taken aback by surprise.

'Oh my word!' She jumped up to her feet looking excited. 'English!' she shrieked excitedly, 'How the hell are you?'

'I'm well thanks Kell,' I answered, 'just happy you're not calling me Kathy or any other name that pops into your head.'

'Oh yeah,' she laughed, 'I remember the evening.' she went on. 'Come sit down next to me, we need to chat, this is a turn up for the books.' She took a swig of wine then continued: 'Half of London's been looking for you!'

I took a moment to consider this unlikeliness, then answered: 'What the hell for Kelly?' slightly worried now, 'I hope you don't mean the police' I added thinking about Kimmi and the little misunderstanding we got into in New York.

'Oh no!' answered Kelly looking at the concern begin to mount on my face, 'It's about a man called Al Cartoon, he owns a small country and such like, but anyway,' she went on, 'apparently you met him once with a view to going on a boat trip to the South of France.'

I felt puzzled for a second, then it all came back to me: 'Oh yeah,' I replied sceptically, 'I know the one.'

'So anyway' she went on, 'rumour has it, a week before the boat was due to leave, you disappeared off the face of the earth, no one could locate you,' she added, 'not for love nor money.'

Oh crap! I thought to myself after hearing her really over emphasise the word money. How much did she really know about the situation and what did she want, more to the point.

'Kelly,' I said hastily thinking how best to play this, 'the trip just wasn't for me, what can I say.'

'It's no big deal.' responded Kelly, 'We just wanted to check you were ok.'

'Oh' I said, not believing a word of it.

'And anyway,' she went on, 'it all worked out for the best in the end.'

'Err, what do you mean Kell?' I said nervously, hoping to God it wasn't anything to do with Money. The thought of them together or anyone with him come to think of it was enough to throw me into a spasm, which is strange as as we know I never really liked him, not enough at any rate.

'Can we smoke in here?' I asked a passing waiter, lighting up before he'd answered me.

Kelly had one too, accompanied by a discreet snort of her gear from under the table and we get back to the conversation.

'So,' went on Kelly nonchalantly, 'that trip was good, I enjoyed it.'

'What trip?' I said in disbelief, 'You didn't go with Al Cartoon? Come on Kelly?'

'Yeah man,' she replied, 'amazing trip English, you really missed out big time there. We had...'

I stopped her there 'Yeah I get the picture Kell. As I said before, it wasn't for me and anyway, what the hell does it have to do with me now, I hardly know the guy.'

'So what?' she interrupted, 'He's dying to meet up with you, he's been waiting all this time, come on, I'll take you round there.'

'Round where?' I said, completely confused now.

'To his house of course,' answered Kelly, 'he's bought a place in London, fat pad too, obviously, he is a prince or whatever.'

'Yeah whatever.' I said, really not feeling this plan of hers.

'Oh come on please, let me take you round there!' she begged, just to see his place and all that, it's seriously the business and anyway,' she said gesturing around her 'do you really want to spend the rest of the evening with this bunch of people?'

Well, I think to myself, looking around me, she did have a point there. 'Where is it?' I said 'Where is his house?'

'Just off Easton Square, you know, near where that art dealer lives, something Sashimi.'

'Oh yeah,' I replied, 'I know the one, right near the Bolivian Embassy with the large gates'.

'Yes,' she said, 'that's the one.'

'How do you know if he's even going to be home?' I added, 'He could be anywhere.'

'But he's not,' she interrupted, 'he's right here in London as we speak.'

I was afraid she was going to say this. 'And anyway,' I added, 'how many times have you seen his house?' I asked her.

She replied with a wink, 'Now that would be telling.' she added.

Well, she did go away with him on a boat I thought to myself, she must know him quite well.

'Ok,' I said to Kelly, 'just a drink ok but no bullshit Kell, honestly, or I'll just leave you there.'

'Ok, ok.' she agreed. 'We better get going soon or it'll be too late to do anything'.

We excused ourselves from the restaurant and headed outside to hail a cab.

'It's 7 45 p.m. now' she went on, 'I'll tell him to expect us around 8.30.'

'Ok' I replied.

Sloane Square. 8.15 p.m.

We exited the cab with Kelly looking the picture of sophistication with a very expensive looking fur draped around her neck, that I had no doubt was bought for her by Cartoon. That was the kind of gift a guy like that would buy you: something showy, ostentatious with no other value than the price tag, a bit like him in my opinion.

I complimented her on the fur, she looked chuffed and told me it was a present. 'Yeah, I figured.' I replied.

We slowly started to make our way around the left hand side of the station where the cab had dropped us. We passed Sloane Avenue and headed towards Easton Square, one of the most sought after addresses in London but images of Money kept flashing through my head. I wished it were him we were going to see, this Al Cartoon guy just didn't do it for me, small country or not.

We arrived at the front door, solid oak, in a warm mahogany shade with a big brass knocker.

'This must be at least a Grade 2 listed building' I remarked to Kelly looking up at its grandness.

'8, 500 sq. feet' she replied, '40 rooms or there about.'

Jees well here goes nothing I thought to myself while Kelly bypassed the knocker in favour of a small bell to the right of the door. She pressed it lightly and my heart started to flutter as uncomfortable memories of our first encounter started to spring to mind, in that all too perfect kitchen of Mimi's under that ridged translucent stair of her and his creepy dancing eyes.

Crap, what am I doing here? But just then it was too late as the door started to open.

I'd not expected him to open the door himself as you could bet your life on the fact he'd have staff around to help him do these menial sorts of things.

He greeted me like one would greet an old lost pall or ex-girlfriend of sorts, not someone he'd only met for barely 20 minutes in some strange lady's kitchen some time previously.

'Hello.' I said a little taken back by his big overly affectionate embrace. 'Great to see you too.' I added, attempting to free myself from his big bear like arms.

'Oooh,' he responded, glancing in Kelly's direction, 'two beautiful ladies on my door step, I am a lucky man!' he added with a smile as we breezed passed him removing our coats for someone to take.

'Don't get too carried away,' I added, giving him a sizable glance, 'it's just a drink.'

But nothing seemed to deter his over-enthusiasm for the situation as he darted like an over-excited puppy to lead the way into his overly elaborate drawing room with exceptional proportions - the drawing room that is, not him. You'd have to ask Kelly about that as I had no intention of finding out how well-proportioned he might or might not be...

'Blimey! Look at the carefully crafted ceilings,' I remarked to no one in particular. 'it's like something out of architectural digest.' I added. This place was massive and oh wow… was that supposed to be him?

Kelly and I were both taken in surprise by an almost life size portrait he had put up of himself, covering almost all of the far side living room wall. 'Wowser!' exclaimed Kelly, 'That's a lot of information there.' she mumbled pointing in the direction of his intimate parts in the painting without even so much of a hint of irony. However, just a glance over at Kelly's dead pan expression and I just couldn't contain myself leading me to let out an almighty laugh.

'That's some picture!' I then offered, by means of explanation for my outburst, managing to compose myself but still not knowing quite what to say or where to look at this point.

I turned to the hallway where one of his - what I presumed to be - house boys was standing.

He instructed the butler to come over to fetch us some drinks. The man/boy kindly obliged with a mini bow of the head and scurried down the hallway to what looked like another set of stairs leading to God knows where but as long as it led to some drinks I didn't really care.

Now it was Al Cartoon's turn to turn to me reaching out one of his particularly creepy long arms and extending it over to me. *Oh Lord have mercy! Where the fuck is Kelly?* I thought looking around, unable to locate her anywhere in the over-sized drawing room. 'We have a cinema room, gym and west facing roof terrace' went on Cartoon proudly. 'Feel free to look around' he added, giving me a long, lingering look. 'Thank you,' I replied, edging away from him ever so slightly.

Right at that moment, the butler person returned with a tray of drinks. Scotch on the rocks for Al Cartoon, and champers with cassis for myself and Kelly who I had no doubt had found her way to a marble clad, chandelier lit bathroom somewhere to administer her daily dose of dusty showbiz. *Oh brilliant!* I thought to myself. *She'll come back buzzing like a fridge and I'll have to make the standard bullshit conversation about things I know nothing about.*

Why was I there? However, hardly giving me a chance to ponder this dilemma, in came Kelly, out of her tits on something or other and ready to party by the look of things. She went to sweep the two glasses off the tray, which was now placed towards the centre of the room on some sort of pouffy thing, and went to shakily hand me the first.

However, obviously underestimating how strong the new batch of coke she picked up was, she had misjudged the gap between myself and the pouffe containing the drinks.

'Damn!' I dived backwards anticipating the tray that was coming towards me in slow motion, but it was too late: the whole thing tipped forward, spraying myself and Kelly with the content of everything on it. I was suddenly wearing a whisky on the rocks, mixed with champagne and cassis as was Kelly, the front of her dress sodden too.

'Oh crickey!' gasped Kelly, 'What the hell happened there?' Jumping back to inspect the damage.

'You're off your tits Kell, that's what!' I offered back in a whispered tone looking around for something to wipe down my dress with. I was however beaten to it and before I knew it Cartoon had rushed over with a handful of napkins from the sideboard and was firmly dabbing them into my chest.

'It's ok,' I said, trying to take the now sodden napkin from him, 'I can manage.' But to my dismay Kelly was now behind me unfastening the zip to my dress, why I didn't know! 'Kell, Kelly!' I repeated trying to get them both away from me. 'It's fine, just leave it. It'll dry' I added, but her and Cartoon obviously had other ideas as Kelly freed the dress from the back of my neck. Cartoon then deliberately let his fingers glide over my now naked chest as the dress went down, only for a split second no less but clearly intentionally all the same.

Kelly then moved round to the front of me, removing her dress also whilst spinning around and bending down slowly to reveal her over exposed arse.

His eyes were glued to her as he reached out to touch her nipples. 'I've been dreaming about this moment' he said, going in to kiss my mouth. His eyes were closed and he was pressed up against me now.

'NO! For God's sake!' I said, pushing him away 'I'm not into this!'

He then turned to Kelly, looking disappointed, but accepting her advances all the same. He then got his hand, sliding it between Kelly's legs, touching her... she moaned out in pleasure, wrapping her arms around his neck and whispering in his ear 'She'll come round' she hissed 'She's a hippie, hippies fuck anything!'

At that moment I snapped, 'Damn you Kelly!' I yelled, grabbing my dress from the floor and slipping it back over my head. She tried to stop me from leaving, touching my arm tenderly. 'Nice try Kell,' I said, moving away from her and edging towards the door, 'but I'm out of here'.

I grabbed my phone, keys and whatever else I'd decided to bring with me (not much usually) and got the hell out of there, leaving Cartoon and Kelly to carry on their little private party without me.

I had no idea how well or how badly Cartoon took my early departure as I had more important things on my mind, like a fucking fashion show I'd been booked to do in Paris in precisely 10 hours' time. I'd totally forgotten about Paris Fashion Week, probably because I'd only booked one show for the whole season and that included shows in London.

I rushed back to the flat at breakneck speed to check my itinerary. *Now let's see... I can't even remember who it's for... oh, here we are...* Solo Samomoto, the Moroccan fashion designer based in Paris (obviously) known for his tailing and avant-garde design aesthetics. Ok, ok, I didn't need to read all this bumf just the time on my Eurostar ticket. Now what time did it say? Crap, it was leaving in 2 hours. I threw a few bits in a bag and made my way to the Eurostar.

Thank God Parisians are not morning people! I thought to myself, I was going to look like crap by the time this train got to the Gare du Nord.

The city took its time to wake up and so did I. On the upside, at least when I'd arrive I would have the streets virtually to myself, shutters down and café counters yet to bustle into life.

I started to make a plan in my head, mainly to keep myself awake during the journey: breakfast at Le Café Marly consisting of a very strong espresso and an uncluttered view of the Louvre iconic glass pyramid before I head off to find my hotel the agency had booked.

The Villa d'Estrees it is on 17 rue Git-le-Coeur. Good, this place is very cool and one of Paris' best boutique hotels. Discreet, chic and basically you can do what you like - my kind of place.

Paris' best kept secret if you ask me.

3 hours later... Paris

I entered the hotel lobby - with only 10 rooms booking was a must - I glanced down at my itinerary: oh very funny, some joker at the agency had booked me in under the name of Anjelica Huston. I looked nothing like Anjelica fucking Huston however the concierge didn't seem to raise an eye brow and showed me to my room. It was small, covered in Moroccan style furnishings.

The first thing I did was to head to the mini bar. I was nervous, I needed a drink.

My show track record was not great. One for Burberry and some other low rent fashion house in New York. However there were bonuses to being at the shitty end of the modelling industry and that was, if you messed up, no one really gave a shit.

The driver the hotel had ordered for me to get to the show was late - the perils of staying at the most relaxed place in the whole of Paris - not that it mattered to me of course, I'd get there when I'd get there, hopefully before the show had finished.

I started to pace round the hotel lobby just to make sure I was in fact, sober enough to walk straight. I got my map out just to see if I could make out where exactly we were going; having no idea which way up it went, this was an impossible task.

Somewhere in the centre it seemed to me... anyway, as soon as the cab rocked up I flung myself in it. 'You know where you're going right?' I asked the driver. He grunted in my direction. *Charming!* I thought to myself, however refraining from saying anything (a first for me) as when I looked over I noticed the mini cab driver only had one arm and I preferred him to keep the other arm on the steering wheel as opposed to around my neck.

The journey was fast as there didn't seem to be any speed limits today (funny that) and we got to the show even before it had started. I was impressed with myself. However the self-congratulating smugness was soon wiped off my face when I caught a glimpse of the shoes I had to wear: *What in God's name were they thinking?* I thought to myself, picking up a free glass of champagne backstage. This was suicidal but it was too late for protestations now. I was third down the runway and the first one had already been down - crap. The makeup artist looked extremely annoyed as she didn't get to make me up like I'd died or something. In breakneck speed I threw on my first outfit which was way too small, oh marvellous... this was going well.

They give me a two minute warning, then a thirty second one then, wait for it, now they gave me the arm signal and I started to walk just like I was on a conveyer belt avoiding the turn at the end. Just as I'd thought I'd get away with it, the heal of my particularly wobbly left shoe began to give way and I felt my rear end pull away from me and head southwards... oh no... this was not supposed to happen...

I didn't remember hitting the ground or the fashion goers scrambling to get me up or, most importantly, out of sight. However I was aware that this would turn out to be my first and last ever show in Paris, or possibly anywhere in the world of fashion.

Well, what could I say... c'est la vie... was there anything to be learnt from the experience? Well, nothing actually except falling off the catwalk hurts. Big time.

October 23rd, 4.45 p.m., Kensington, London.

Listening to 'Ready to Go' - Republica

London is cold, wet and unforgiving on my return, a bit like my mood really, so it was back to the bullshit routine of mundane living, for now anyway.

I went to my appointments reasonably on time and generally towed the line. I even got a dog called Gruffy from the local drug dealer that lived next door. He must have been doing well to live in Chelsea I thought to myself until the police came round to bust him one Sunday early hours during one of their pre-dawn raids.

That's how I got the dog you see as he was unable to take her to prison with him.

She was a silly little dog, of no fixed breed. Small in size with a long fluffy tail, Christ knew where he got her from but I liked her. She was cool, street smart too. However most described her as looking like a rat and sounding like a seal but it didn't bother me, she was my companion.

Only once did we have a hiccup on one of our days out when her right paw got stuck in the escalator coming up from the tube station on exit from Oxford Circus. I had to take her to the R.S.P.C.A. the next day to have her paw stitched up but apart from that she was fine. In fact the only people not so keen on her were the agency as she poo pooed on the floor once in the office but fuck'em, I cleaned it up.

Thursday 24th October, mid-afternoon, London

I was off to the Gloucester Arms on Sloane Street, my latest watering hole.

Rebel and Dark were to join me down there which was a small miracle really as drinking in the Knightsbridge area of town was really not their thing, nor mine come to think of it, however this pub was not like most. They said it was traditionally English but really it was not anything of the sort as very few English people could afford to live in these parts any more, making it nobody's local.

Wealthy foreigners had never had a pub culture so they bypassed this place too, making it extremely quiet. This in turn kept the prices down hence the reason we frequented this place (it was cheap).

Propping up the bar, I ordered myself a white wine spritzer. Not my usual drink of choice, however it was not yet evening and later on today I had promised Douglas in New York I'd call him and arrange my return trip before it got to Christmas.

I wonder how Kimmi is doing I thought to myself. We'd not spoken since Mexico City and that was coming up to a while ago now. I put my drink down and searched for a cig, last Marlboro Light in there, I knew it. I found the pack and located my big novelty pack of matches. *Why do I always carry these?* I thought to myself, they were more suited to lighting candles in the home then what I used them for. Old habits die hard.

I made my way out the front of the pub to have a quick smoke and a nose down Sloane Street.

Out of nowhere it seemed I felt a tap on my left shoulder. I spun around in haste to see who it was and ended up gasping in surprise and dropping my bag to the floor.

'Hey Kid, I bought you that bag.' the man's voice said. 'I bought you that bag for your birthday, all that time back on Sloane Avenue, Saturday afternoon 4pm. I remember everything. You wanted it so badly and it was extremely overpriced.' He added with a wink and a smile.

'MONEY!' I said jumping up and giving him a squeeze. 'Wow! I thought I'd never see you again!' I blurted 'and… and…' I said, looking for the words 'I've been thinking about you.'

'Oh have you?' he said astonished, 'I suppose I've missed you too' he added in surprise. 'I mean' he went on, 'how could anyone not miss you?' he said with a small laugh.

'I won't answer that' I said outing my cig and making my way down Sloane Street together with Money, completely forgetting I'd arranged to meet Dark and Rebelstar back in the pub.

'I'm getting out of the fashion game' I announced to him, 'It's not for me anymore' I went on. 'I need to broaden my horizons' I added looking serious.

'I couldn't agree more,' he replied putting an arm around my shoulder, 'but what will you do?' he asked, looking slightly concerned.

'I'm not quite sure yet' I answered, 'but I'm thinking about becoming a writer, what do you think?' I asked putting an arm around his waist.

We stopped walking for a second. 'Well English he said, I think you'll make a terrific writer. However,' he went on, 'I don't want you writing about me.'

'Oh!' I said with a laugh and a smile 'don't worry about that, and anyway,' I then cleared my throat for dramatic effect, 'it was never about the Money!' and with that I kissed him like I meant it, well, for the first time ever.

He looked at me in surprise, 'And fools dance' he added with a laugh, 'but only on Sloane Street!'

Made in the USA
Lexington, KY
19 July 2014